MW00780502

JULIET DIES TWICE

Persons this *Mystery* is about—

MILLICENT LEGG,
a very small young woman, peers up through thick glasses, wears
braces on her teeth, and has one of those sullen skins that look ready
to break out into acne under your very eyes.

EUDORA YORK,
twenty-two years old, has a square face, eyes which turn upward
at the outer corners, and a profile which is imperious and wise.

PROFESSOR BREWER,
of the department of Abnormal Psychology, has a pointed face,
topped by a wide dome of forehead, and always wears a faint flush,
as though he might at any moment explode with some gnawing internal anger or provoking private joke.

ANN LAIRD,
a small dark thing with sparkling amber eyes and shiny mahogany
hair. Her talent comes first with Ann—she can no more help that than
she can help breathing.

AMES HANNA,
a young man with a magnificent array of white teeth, springy black
hair, shiny hazel eyes that have never cried a tear, and that grin!

JIM LAIRD,
a tall blond man with an arc of straight tan hair hanging down over
a wide forehead. This, with the cornsiik eyebrows and sandy lashes,
gives his face a boyish look.

PROFESSOR ROMAINE,
a gray-haired woman of delightful individuality. Her forceful dark
eyes indicate that she was once very beautiful.

DAVE DRASKA,
a tall, skinny, catty Russian. He has a long thin neck, narrow eyes,
and unctuous hair.

MEG FIFE,
a restrained girl, has one of those clear, fine voices. She is small,
but she has big feet. Very big feet. And her ankles escape being
thick by a sixteenth of an inch.

LIEUTENANT RICHARD TUCK,
of the Homicide Squad, is a giant with seal-brown hair. His skin is
the color of a well-smoked meerschaum pipe, his eyes the color of
black coffee, and his long face as expressionless as a statue.

CLYDE BILLINGS,
a small young man, unmarried. He believes he is the greatest musician in the world.

PAUL OBER,
a man with a handsome face, muscular co-ordination that makes his
every motion on stage an unconscious masterpiece of timing, and
one of those voices that take any line and make it unforgettable.
And he is exactly five feet five inches tall.

JULIET DIES TWICE

Things this *Mystery* is about—

A silver VIAL . . .

A KEY . . .

A 5x7" NOTEBOOK . . .

A frozen FISH . . .

A convertible COUPE . . .

A brass TRAY . . .

A pair of black RUBBERS . . .

Five cigarette BUTTS . . .

An iron DUMBBELL . . .

A *LIEUTENANT TUCK* MURDER MYSTERY

JULIET
DIES
TWICE

By LANGE LEWIS

Author of "Meat for Murder," and
"Murder Among Friends."

Author's Dedication—
For GRACE W. LAVAYEA

WILDSIDE PRESS

JULIET DIES TWICE

List of *Exciting* Chapters—

Juliet Dies Twice

Chapter One: WE KNOW NOT WHAT WE MAY BE

HEAT MADE a mild mirage on the road far ahead; water seemed to be lying thin against the tar. The square face of the young woman at the wheel of the open car was stern and calm below the dark glasses which tilted upward at the outer corners, like the eyes beneath them.

The very small young woman who seemed to be making an effort to occupy as little as possible of the remainder of seat was not looking at the road, but at the profile of the driver, imperious and wise, thrusting forward from the backward flow of straight brown hair.

Millicent is watching me, thought the girl at the wheel. *She's feeling small and helpless beside me; she enjoys feeling small and helpless.*

Eudora thought, *Millicent has one of those sullen skins that look ready to break out into acne under your very eyes.* She said, "If it's too hot for you we can stop and put the top up. You look a little like an ad for sunburn lotion."

"Oh, no," said Millicent urgently. "I wouldn't think of causing all that trouble. I'm not a bit too warm."

Eudora gave another quick sideways glance. Millicent's eyes, large and brown behind her thick glasses, seemed to protrude a little more than usual. Her dun-colored hair was tired and dusty, and small beads of sweat were clustered in the central hollow of her upper lip—just short enough to reveal the silver gleam of her dental braces. There was a dull, baked flush on her cheekbones.

"If you'd really rather wait for a sunstroke it's all right with me," said Eudora.

"I was simply thinking," said Millicent, with miniature dignity, "that there isn't much time."

Oh, Lord, thought Eudora, *she makes you feel like such a heel!* She said, "Well, darling, we only have ten minutes, so if you're sure you can stand it—"

Millicent beamed at the *darling* and immediately set herself the task of looking brave.

With a conscious effort, Eudora wrenched Millicent's presence from her mind and looked from the road to the Southern California countryside, watching for the low white buildings that were their destination. She saw them in a few minutes, staring at the road across wide green lawns, backed by the hazy folds of mountains. She turned into the private drive leading off the highway, drove as far as a cement pathway reaching across the wide rolling lawn to the largest of the buildings, and parked in the blue shadow of a pepper tree. She dropped her keys into her purse and turned in the seat to confront Millicent, who was making futile dabs at her hair with a very small comb.

"*Comb* it, Millicent," she found herself saying with absurd irritation. "You look like the White Queen!"

"I *am* combing it," Millicent keened.

Eudora thought, *You could make a sadist out of Elsie Dinsmore, my girl. A person says something mean without volition, like swatting a fly that sits too long within reach.*

She got out of the car. "Do you want to chuck your books into the turtle?"

Millicent shook her head a trifle sulkily.

The chromium handle of the turtle was so hot it burned Eudora's hand. She raised the lid quickly and deposited two thick textbooks in the huge maw.

"We'd better hurry," Millicent called.

That's another thing about Millicent, thought Eudora, and dropped the lid with a bang. Returning to the side of the car, she found her gathering an amazing number of bobby pins from her pink skirt. "Were all those in your hair?" she asked.

"Oh, yes," said Millicent.

"*Exactly* like the White Queen," Eudora muttered, and closed her eyes against the heat. She became conscious of the prolonged snick of a lawnmower. There was summer in the sound. She opened her eyes just in time to see the car door swing outward and a size-one saddle-top oxford reach for the ground. Then she and Millicent stepped from the shade into the white glare of June sunlight, and started up the walk that led to the insane asylum.

A man in a gray sweat shirt and dingy cord trousers was bearing toward them from the direction of the building, cut grass spraying out each side of his lawnmower.

"I don't know whether I'm going to like this," Millicent remarked, making very apparent efforts to keep up with Eudora's long strides. Eudora forced herself not to lengthen her step and said nothing. Millicent tried again. "I don't suppose we'll be shown any really dangerous inmates." Her voice was somewhere between fear and eagerness.

"There may be a murderer or two."

"Oh!"

Just as Eudora became aware that the lawnmower had stopped, Millicent clutched her arm for the second time that day. "Look at his feet!" she whispered.

Just ahead of them, the man in the sweat shirt was mopping his forehead. He had on rubbers. They were bright black, and Eudora could see cut slivers of grass clinging to their sleekness. As her eyes met his, an unremarkable gray in an unremarkable face, the man put away his handkerchief, lowered his head and pushed the lawnmower doggedly past them.

"Rubbers!" whispered Millicent, staring after him. "On a day like this!"

"He may have been watering the lawn."

Millicent said, "Of course! How silly of me. For just

a minute I thought he was one of the inmates."

"He probably is. Good occupational therapy, gardening."

"You mean they let lunatics run around mowing the lawn!"

"Millicent, you've had almost a semester of Abnormal Psychology. Are you still *afraid* of lunatics?"

"Yes," said Millicent. "Aren't you?"

"But why?" The main difference between sanity and insanity is simply degree. Lunatics often show the same peculiarities normal people do, only more so."

"I don't see anything very reassuring in that," said Millicent, bluntly. Then she abruptly changed the subject. "Look!" she said into Eudora's ear. "There's Joe and Bob. And Norm. Don't you think he's aristocratic-looking?"

Eudora said nothing, but smiled a little.

Millicent went on with her catalogue. "And there's Professor Brewer. I hope he doesn't say something sarcastic. We *are* late."

Professor Brewer glanced over toward them.

"Don't you think he has marvelous eyes?" asked Millicent.

"And he has pants, too," said Eudora.

Millicent displayed hurt feelings all the way to the door of the asylum where the rest of the class was waiting.

Professor Brewer was surrounded by a group of wide-eyed women students to whom he was speaking in his jerky voice. His pointed face, topped by a wide dome of forehead, always wore a faint flush, rather as though he might at any moment explode with some gnawing internal anger or provoking private joke. Today he was really red, and his greenish eyes glittered restlessly. *Almost as though he were blushing*, Eudora decided. *That is, if he could.*

"Freud," Professor Brewer was saying, "thinks that the **delusion of grandeur** involves a secondary narcissism, with inflation of the ego due to the withdrawal of the libido from natural objects."

Out of sheer dislike, Eudora decided to interrupt him. "Professor Brewer," she called.

His mouth open to start another sentence, he turned toward her quickly. "Yes?"

"Don't you think," asked Eudora innocently, "that Freud attaches too much significance to the sexual content of dreams?"

Knowing full well that Freud's entire dream theory had its foundations in frustration of the sexual impulse, a fact which Brewer had dwelt on for several lectures, considerably hampered by the fact that he was teaching in a coeducational university, Eudora felt that the question was well calculated to annoy. It did.

Brewer for a moment simply stared. His face seemed to get a little more flushed. "But, my dear young woman," he said at last, in a voice as cold as his appearance was warm, "that is the entire basis of his theory!"

"I'm afraid I didn't quite gather that from your lectures," Eudora said, sweetly and submissively.

"My lectures," said Professor Brewer, very gently, "were, I think, reasonably clear?"

"Oh, I didn't mean *that!*" said Eudora.

Before Brewer could say more, a male nurse in white duck trousers and a short-sleeved white jacket was at his elbow, murmuring something. There was a brief conference, during which Brewer looked extremely wise, nodding and grinning conspiratorially. Then he turned, faced the class and spoke briskly. "All right. In you go. On your final examination you will be held responsible for everything you see here today. Don't be afraid of hurting the inmates' feelings. You can't. Ask all the questions you want, but spare my blushes by displaying as little ignorance as possible."

The class moved like a big, slow, gaudy ameba into the

house of darkness.

When they came out of the building at last, their shadows were long on the grass. The gala mood was gone, and in its place was silence and wonder.

"It's so terrible!" burst out Millicent, when she and Eudora were halfway down the walk. "I'm sorriest for the woman who thought Marlene Dietrich was jealous of her. She was so *ugly*."

"That may have been the beginning of her delusion," Eudora said. "The gnawing need not to believe in her own ugliness. How? By nurturing the belief that a beautiful woman hated her. You perhaps noticed that, apart from her delusion, she spoke quite normally."

Millicent shuddered. "Yes. That made it much worse."

"There's that matter of degree again," said Eudora. "Why, I can think of several people with mild delusions of grandeur. Take your pal Ann Laird. She knows she's good. It's not a logical conviction. She just *knows*. And when she gets on stage, that knowledge helps her to turn out a swell performance."

Millicent pressed her lips firmly together. "Ann is the most modest person I know."

"Except where her delusion is concerned," said Eudora, opening the door of the car. "Ann's delusion doesn't lead her into antisocial actions, so she's sweating in Touchstone Theater today, and not up here."

"I don't like your theory," said Millicent.

"And I know someone," went on Eudora, and heard the emptiness in her own voice as she spoke, "to whom life has been so damnably, eternally bountiful that he believes that nothing unpleasant can ever happen to him. And that comes close to being a delusion, too."

"You mean Ames," observed Millicent, sagely.

"I mean Ames," said Eudora, and jammed the key into the ignition with unnecessary force.

On the outskirts of Los Angeles they stopped at a drive-in and ordered cokes. Millicent sucked the cool liquid up the straw as greedily as a child, stopped, sighed, and said, "I'm glad you brought up Freud's dream theory. I couldn't quite believe all that either."

Eudora decided that it would involve too much effort to explain to Millicent that she had not been panning Freud, for whom she had profound respect, but Brewer, for whom she had none at all.

"I had a dream last night," said Millicent, her eyes fixed on the windshield while she gathered remembered fragments in her mind. "It was a funny dream, and had nothing to do with sex. I don't know what it meant."

"Very interesting," said Eudora.

"I dreamed," said Millicent, "I was at that advertising agency where Jim Laird works. The room was empty, and it seemed to be very early in the morning. I was sitting near Jim's desk. On the drawing board was a pencil sketch of Beethoven. It was very good. He got the essence of that strong, brooding face with the almost brutal mouth. Then —the door opened, and a janitor pushed in a big corrugated box, cut down in front, and Jim was sitting in a sort of seat in it. He smiled at me, and the janitor went away, and Jim tried to stand up, but his legs were paralyzed. I had to help him out of the box. When I took his arm, there was a sort of electric shock, and when it went away, he was looking down at his legs in a funny way. Then he stepped out of the box and smiled at me again and went over to his desk."

"Very interesting," said Eudora, meaning it this time. She thought, *The drawing of Beethoven stood for the love of music that is probably the only interest Milly and Jim Laird have in common. The fact that they were alone in the office, and that the menial who pushed him went away at once, but particularly the fact that he was in the box, stand for her subconscious desire to have Jim for herself. The paralysis means she wants to be necessary to him; she wants to be in a position to help him. The electric shock probably symbolizes a love affair between them. And his ability to use his legs after she touched him undoubtedly was an expression of her subconscious belief that she could be a good influence on him if she had the chance.* She faced Millicent's absorbed stare. "Millicent darling, are you in love with Jim Laird?"

"My best friend's husband? You have a terrible mind!" stated Millicent in an outraged whisper.

Eudora dropped a quarter to the tray and honked for the waitress. "No, dear," she said quietly. "You have. A perfectly terrible unconscious mind, just like all the rest of us." She backed the car. "Full of strange desires that never see the light of day. Full of powerful wishes that will always masquerade through your dreams. Don't feel too badly about it."

But Millicent did. She sat very still, with her hands clasped in her lap, her lips firmly shut, and ignored Eudora with great intensity all the way home.

The sun was setting when they neared the campus.

"We've missed dinner," Millicent said, remotely.

The prospect of eating dinner with Millicent was not pleasing to Eudora. When you have shared the same small room with a person for nearly a year, the absence of that person for a short time is not unwelcome.

"I'll let you·off at the Wagon Wheel. I'll have to dash across to the theater. I'm on props for the show."

They reached University Avenue, which was to Southwest University both heart and bloodstream, by a side street that ended almost directly across from Old College. The central portion had been built in the '80's and had tall, austere windows and a four-sided tower at the left front corner, topped by an elongated pyramid of dullish green. Two sprawling wings had been added to the original structure, and the whole had been stuccoed over with leaden gray, over which vines grew. There was a look of bats to the tower, and the elms rearing from the wide lawn around it were motionless as painted trees. Seeing it, Millicent forgot to be hurt. "Look, Eudora!"

"Old College. It was right there this morning."

Millicent didn't even hear her. "I never see it at this time of day without being tremendously impressed, the way you are impressed sometimes by the face of a very old woman. One so old that all her friends are dead, and perhaps even her children. She doesn't remember them, except once in a long while, remotely."

The simile attracted Eudora. Recognizing a genuine emotion, and realizing that she had not been kind to Millicent, she had the grace to fall in with her mood. So she quoted from Stevenson, one of Millicent's favorite authors: *"There are some old houses that demand to be haunted; there are some dark gardens that cry aloud for murder. . . ."*

Millicent's lips were parted, her eyes were glued on the building. Eudora swung around the corner as Millicent asked, "Is that what it makes you think of, Eudora?"

"That," said Eudora, "and psychology class at nine in the morning." She came to a neat stop in front of the Wagon Wheel café.

Chapter Two: TOO RASH, TOO SUDDEN

SHE WENT up the dozen stone steps leading to the long porch of Old College two at a time and tried first the tall brown oak double door labeled *Touchstone Theater* in black letters. It was locked, so she turned and made for the main entrance to the building, which faced the head of the steps, and which was also a tall brown double door, one half of which stood open. There was a quick footfall from the gloomy corridor beyond, and suddenly Ames was standing in the open doorway, one arm propping his weight against the jamb, his head cocked alertly.

She came to an abrupt stop and stood facing him.

He smiled at her, showing a magnificent array of white teeth, and said, "How about some chow?"

Her heart was pounding from her race up the steps, but what made her unable to speak was the unbelievable insolence of the figure before her. That perfect tweed coat, silk open-necked shirt, springy black hair that always looked as though it had just had a shower—and that grin! And those narrow, shiny hazel eyes that had never cried a tear.

"You look like the devil," said Ames. "I told you once that white's not at all your color. You're too sallow."

"Jaundice," said Eudora. "Runs in my family. We like it. May I pass?"

Ames, still smiling, shook his head slowly.

"Ames," said Eudora, "turn off that grin and let me pass. I'm late."

He continued to shake his head. So she turned her back on him and started down the steps. She had descended two when he was in front of her. He took a quick, careful grasp on both her wrists and said, with an absurd imitation of chagrin, "Don't you love me any more?"

Struggling to free her wrists, she pulled as far away from him as she could. "We've been all over that. No, I don't. I mean, I never did. *Let go!*"

"May I pass?" asked a deep and completely uninterested voice behind them. She tipped up her head and saw Professor Romaine standing just above them, looking very impeccable in her brown suit and severe brown hat. Her smile had a deliberate vagueness to it, and her dark eyes met Eudora's and then slid sideways, as though looking for escape from embarrassment.

"Certainly," said Ames glibly, and stepped aside.

Professor Romaine passed, as a queen might have passed, and Eudora felt small and noisy and slightly indecent.

Ames looked up at her. "I'll make a scene, you know."

"That's what I should be doing," she said coldly. "Do you see that bulletin board?"

Ames looked toward the door to the theater. "Yes."

"What does it say?"

"It says *Romeo and Juliet*, and there are a lot of photographs."

"And do you see the opening date?"

"June tenth."

"That's tomorrow night. And the balcony isn't finished yet. And I'm on props. Get it?"

"Oh?" said Ames. He frowned. "I was going to take you to a little spot on the Strip. Well, I'll compromise. We'll go to the Derby on Wilshire."

"You're not going to get away with it!" Eudora said through her teeth, jerking against his firm grasp.

"Florida was a bust," said Ames conversationally. "Tremendous hotels, and a lotta sea and beach and sky. Some swell-looking women, too, but—" he sighed elaborately,— "no Eudora."

"Were there crocodiles?"

"Yes."

She sighed. "But none of them ate you." She gave him a level look. "That's what I kept dreaming all the while you were gone. Every night you got eaten by a crocodile, and I always woke up laughing."

"Shall I tell you what I kept dreaming, Eudora *dear?*"

"No!"

There was a shuffle of feet from inside the building, and the crisp sound of feet on cement. Three boys in paint-splashed overalls thudded down the steps, all turning to look at Eudora, and then at her tightly grasped wrists. "Hello, York," said the sandy one. "We're knocking off for dinner. Try to show up about seven, huh?"

"All right, Joe."

Ames said, "That doesn't give us much time."

"Pal," she said, "we don't have any time, none, not one little single minute."

Ames's face lighted up. "I know what. I'll carry you to the car!" And he scooped her up in his arms.

She forced herself not to kick foolishly. "All right. Put me down. I'll come."

He set her on her feet, still keeping a firm hold on one wrist. She scowled at him, at the long black Cadillac parked illegally in the red zone in front of Old College, and especially at the beating of her own heart.

The Brown Derby was a brown derby, of painted stucco, with wings. The food was good, but expensive. The headwaiter, who also looked expensive, piloted them toward the inner café, but Ames nodded toward the glassed-in patio. The waiter led them to a miniature covered wagon of blue canvas with a table in front of it. Looking at the cozy intimacy of the covered wagon, Eudora said, "Let's have something right out in the open, Ames—cooler, you know." The waiter, with no change of expression, seated them at a round white metal table with a yellow umbrella.

Ames eyed his menu and said. "We'll have two martinis to start with—"

"One martini," corrected Eudora.

"—and do you have any Château d'Yquem?"

The headwaiter was regretful. While they conferred over the wine list, Eudora looked steadily at Ames and saw him in 10 years. with jowls beginning to droop, going aimlessly from place to place, ordering the best wines with his father's money.

"What would you like to eat?" he asked, bending toward her with a solicitude that was a deliberate imitation. like so many of his actions.

"Ham," said Eudora. "And the chef's salad

"Ham," confided Ames to the waiter. "I'll have the brook trout, if they're good."

"Oh, very good." The waiter left.

Ames leaned forward and spoke confidingly. "I don't know what I see in you, Eudora. You're not terribly pretty, and your figure is—well—fair. Sometimes I think it's your eyes. They slant just a little. And then again I think it may be your gams. You have nice gams."

"Shut up about my gams, please."

"All right." He lowered his eyes a trifle. "I'll talk about your beautiful, round—"

"Ames," she said, in a deadly tone.

The martinis came. Eudora looked down at hers—pale yellow crystal with an olive heart. She ate the olive. She said, "I have never been more bored."

Ames shook his head. "I don't know what I see in you."

Something warm burst in her head. "I'll tell you, shall I? You don't really see anything at all. You pretend to—because it amuses you not to have something you want. The only reason I held your interest for one moment is because you'd heard I didn't care much for men. You were sure I'd care for you. I didn't. And ever since, for eight long months, you've found fun trying to make me care."

"You do care," he said flatly.

"I don't!"

"Do!"

She saw he was making a child's argument of it and relaxed. *I mustn't let him get me angry,* she told herself. The ham was laid before her.

Eating his brook trout with deftness, Ames said, "I know what I see in you. Shall I tell you?" He took a sip of wine; she didn't answer, so he went on, "I was in a museum once, when I was a little boy, in the room with the mummies."

"And ever since you've been searching for a woman with that decayed look."

"And in the room with the mummies was a bust of an Egyptian queen, and she was beautiful. She had a long neck, and a proud square chin, and she was a lovely golden brown. And her tall headdress was painted blue and gold, and her lips were the color of blood. Her eyes were long and painted and—and secret. They could have been the eyes of a person terribly wise, or the eyes of an imbecile. You couldn't guess which, and you wanted to know."

"Did you ever find out?" asked Eudora politely.

"You've got what she had. You've got something secret inside you that you don't show anyone, and I want it. I want to know you, Eudora."

"That's really wonderful," she said. "You could do a story about it, or a popular song—"

"Someday," he said, "I'm going to kill you."

"How much of that was true? I'm really curious."

"None of it," he said agreeably. "I made it up as I went along."

But oddly enough, she didn't believe him. And then she caught a sly glint in his eye, and knew she was falling into his trap. "You're so slippery," she said.

"You haven't touched your ham," he reminded her.

Chagrined, she ate steadily for several minutes.

"So tonight," Ames remarked, "we're going to Mexico. We'll be married in one of those picturesque little churches—"

"When I marry you," she said, "the stars will stand still in their courses."

"Quite poetic, dear."

She put down her fork with a clatter. "I hate you."

He looked aggrieved, but his eyes were dancing. He rested his chin in his hand and said, "Tell me more."

"You're really fantastic, like a character out of a story written in the late 1920's. You're out of style. You're aimless and foppish and sure of yourself because nothing's ever gone wrong for you that money—your father's money —couldn't mend. God help you when it does, because you'll crumble. You'll collapse. Listen to me. Even talking about you I sound like a slick story myself."

She slid her chair back, but before she was on her feet, he'd risen also and beckoned the waiter. She went past him fast but out of the corner of her eye saw him drop a bill to the table, seize the wine bottle. "I'll just take this along," she heard him say to the waitress.

Just as she reached the entrance a yellow taxi drew up out front and disgorged a clot of talking people. She saw them give the driver money and move toward her. She ran past them, jumped into the cab and slammed the door. "Hurry!" she commanded. The driver took her at her word and started away so rapidly that she was hurled against the back cushion of the seat.

She twisted around and peered out of the rear window. Ames was standing looking after the taxi. Then he raised the bottle of wine high in the air and with a quick downward drive of his arm smashed it in the gutter

Chapter Three: ASSOCIATION TEST

THE ABNORMAL Psychology class met in a sunless second-floor lecture room at the rear of Old College. The seats were tiered, and Eudora sat at the end of the top row, chin in hand, looking out a long narrow window at the grassy oval of the practice field in back of the building where a boy in a maroon sweater stood with his head bent over a stop watch, while one sprinter circled the track. Around and around, like her thoughts.

She heard Professor Brewer's quick, cold voice saying, "I am going to conduct an experiment this morning which I hope will clarify some doubts about the efficiency of the association-test method in revealing the content of the subject's mind, in spite of resistance on his part."

She thought, *I'd like to try that on Ames.*

Professor Brewer pointed to a metronome on his desk.

"This will time the interval between the stimulus word, which I shall give, and the response word, which the subject will give. I will explain further when I have chosen the two subjects." He walked to his desk and picked up two sealed white envelopes. He held one aloft, and those wet brilliant eyes of his roved the room, settled on Eudora. "Miss York!" he said briskly, with an imperious gesture of the envelope.

Eudora stood up and walked down to Professor Brewer's desk. He handed her the envelope without looking at her, and raising the other envelope called, "Miss Legg!" Millicent's tiny, pop-eyed face rose abruptly above the turned heads. When Millicent was standing beside Eudora, he looked from one to the other and then spoke above their heads to the class. "You will each follow the directions you will find inside these envelopes. You will return to class in exactly ten minutes. Good-by." As they reached the door he called, "Kindly do not compare instructions."

So they stood, one on each side of the closed door, and opened their envelopes. Eudora's contained a key, another smaller envelope, and a typewritten note: "*Go to the prop room in the basement of Old College. Open the door. Then open the other envelope.*"

She and Millicent walked silently down the stairs together. Millicent said good-by in an uncertain way and walked along the gloomy first-floor hall toward the hot brightness of the stone porch of Old College. Eudora turned toward the rear of the building and continued down the wooden staircase to the basement.

The corridor to the prop room was at right angles with the one corresponding to the main corridor on the first floor. Both were lined with green metal lockers which had not been used for many years. The basement was dark until she pushed the button of the ancient switch at the foot of the stairs. When she came to the tall brown door of the prop room, she tried it, but it was locked. So she used the old-fashioned key which Professor Brewer had so thoughtfully provided and pushed the door open. It squeaked.

In the dim light that struggled through the two frosted-glass windows, one on each side of another door which opened onto the grass and elm trees at the side of Old College, she saw a girl in a white dress on the floor beside a huge, tin-topped table on which flats were often laid for painting. A dark splotch, darker than the dusty floor, had spread out from beneath her head.

It took a moment for the shock to leave her. Then she saw Brewer's plan. Millicent had been sent on some innocent errand. The same association test would be given both of them, and the class would be asked to judge which had seen a good imitation of a dead body.

She stepped closer and saw that Brewer had chosen his star wisely. It was Ann Laird, her amber eyes fixed on the ceiling, her face powdered to a whiteness that was most effective in the artificial twilight of the room. Remembering the other envelope, she opened it and drew out a folded sheet of typing paper. By peering closely, she made out the typing—in red: *The murderess is named Eudora York.*

That gave her more of a start than the body had. "It seems that I done you in," she commented to Ann.

Ann didn't move a muscle.

"O.K., Ann. Don't take any wooden lilies."

Ann seemed to smile faintly at that, and satisfied at having forced her out of character for a moment, Eudora turned and shut the door. Then, with a grin, she locked it and went down the hall under the naked electric-light bulbs, pushed the switch and thudded up the stairs.

One of the words will be blood, she thought. *I'll give him "red"—that's innocuous enough. Then he'll spring "murder." I'll say—let me see—"Macbeth."*

The class turned expectant faces toward her as she

opened the door to the lecture room. Millicent was not back yet. "I'll begin with you," Brewer said, and started the metronome, beside which lay his watch. He indicated the chair beside his desk and she sat down, determined to fight every key word.

It went very much as she had expected. He shot a word at her from the list before him on his desk. The metronome ticked twice before she replied. The door opened and Millicent came in, looking vaguely alarmed. "Sit down there, Miss Legg," Professor Brewer commanded, pointing to a vacant seat at the end of the first row.

"Death!" said Professor Brewer. Three ticks. "Taxes," said Eudora. She heard several titters. Brewer penned a neat "3" beside the word.

"Head!" The word "blood" came swiftly and inexorably to her lips, but she forced it back. "Ache."

"Green."—"Grass."

"Water."—"Rubbers."

Then it came. "Dead." Four ticks. There was only one word in her mind, and that was "girl." She mustn't take too long. That would be admission of resistance. "Ducat!"

"Did you say duck?" asked Professor Brewer, although she was certain he had heard perfectly.

"I said 'ducat.'"

He looked politely dubious. *He's not playing fair*, she thought resentfully. She said, "When Hamlet kills Polonius he says, 'Dead for a ducat.'"

"Oh," said Professor Brewer, immensely relieved. "I see. Well, well. Bread."

"Did you say bread?" asked Eudora politely.

"I did."—"Butter."

"Needle."—"Pin."

"Lamp."—"Light."

"Frog."—"Bull."

"Finger."—"Thumb."

"Wound."—"Blood." It came out before she could stop

herself.

"Carrot."—"Diamond."

"Hm," murmured Brewer. "Expensive tastes."

He got his laugh and then said, "Glass."— "Dark." She realized she was thinking of those dirty windows of the prop room.

The list went on. She had a little trouble with "floor." She almost said, "Body," but came through after only three ticks of the metronome with "mop," at which Brewer murmured, "Domestic, too."

Tension grew in her as the test went on, but she went to her seat with the conviction that Brewer was having a stiff struggle to mask his irritation.

Millicent, sitting very stiffly in the straight chair Eudora had just vacated, looked unwaveringly at Brewer, rather as though he had hypnotized her. But she came out with fairly standard answers until Brewer said, "Glass." Millicent said, "Beer." The class chuckled. And again, a little later, Brewer said, "Bed." Millicent opened her mouth to reply. Then she closed it and flushed a deep, anguished pink. The class howled. Millicent, apparently not conscious of it, said, "Post!" loudly and firmly. The next word was unfortunate in its connection. Eudora wondered if he had done it on purpose. "Love." But the answer was swift and matter-of-fact and stifled further laughter. "Hate," said Millicent.

When Millicent had returned to her seat, Professor Brewer said, "As I have told you, one of these two students went across the street and drank a Coca-Cola. The other went to the properties room downstairs and saw what I hope looked like a dead body. She received, I think, a little additional shock on reading a note which stated she was the murderess. The chief purpose of that note was to put her subconsciously on her guard. You will each write on a slip of paper the name of the student you think saw the body."

While that was being done, Professor Brewer became absorbed in a book. In a few minutes he looked up, hurried a group who had their heads together in discussion, and then collected the papers himself. He swiftly tabulated the results on the board under the headings *"Legg,"* *"York."* Eudora won, by 14 votes.

"Would you like to tell us about your experience in the basement, Miss York?" asked Professor Brewer.

A little heady with her failure, Eudora said, "Gimme another chance, and I know I can get away with it!"

Then the bell pealed loud and imperious, and class was over. As the students thumped down the aisle and shuffled in a close-packed herd through the door, Brewer called, "Don't forget to give me the key, Miss York."

As Eudora laid it down next to the metronome, she couldn't resist a last word. "I hope you gave *her* a key, because I locked the door when I left."

Brewer looked up from the papers he was sorting. Two lines of puzzlement carved themselves between his dark eyebrows. "Her?" he asked, blankly.

Chapter Four: THIS FAIR CORPSE

No, THOUGHT Eudora, standing beside Ann Laird, *That's not ketchup.* And then she had what was very nearly a hallucination. Quite clearly she heard her own voice say, "Don't take any wooden lilies." Before she realized that the voice was nothing but auditory memory inside her own head, she shivered a little, *What made me think she smiled?* she wondered vacantly, and all at once her knees melted, and she wanted to sit down.

"I don't understand this," Brewer was saying, in a muffled tone that was unlike his usual assured, jerky way of talking. The relationship of teacher and student seemed to have disappeared, and Eudora thought of his part in this make-believe that was something very real.

She looked at him. "Neither do I," she said slowly.

He was looking down at those dead amber eyes. "It should have been Barney Noble—that's who you should have found. I arranged the whole thing with him Wednesday after class."

"Let me get it straight. Ann Laird had no part in the experiment?"

A little life seeped into Brewer's voice. "No part at all. I scarcely knew the girl's name."

A sudden picture flashed into Eudora's brain. Last night. The dress rehearsal. Brewer, standing in the doorway to Touchstone Theater, watching Ann Laird play Juliet. And on his face a look of complete absorption.

She saw another picture—Barney Noble, a sturdy column of tanned neck rising from a letterman's maroon sweater, as slow in class as he was fast on the football field, saying, "She may be Sarah Bernhardt to you but she's just one cute baby to me." They had all laughed, there on the porch of Old College, and Ann Laird, passing by below, had heard the laughter and had turned her head—quickly so that shiny mahogany hair swirled on the sunlit air—and smiled up at them.

"Yes? It should have been Barney Noble?"

"I asked him to stay after class on Wednesday. I told him my scheme. He said he'd buy a bottle of ketchup and do it up brown. We went to the Drama Office and I explained to the secretary there that I'd need two keys to the prop room, and why. She gave me a key to the inner door and a key to the outer. I gave that one to Barney so no one would see him coming in through the building this morning. Then I went to my office and typed the notes for you and what's-her-name. Naturally, when Barney didn't come to class this morning, I assumed he was down here with his bloody ketchup."

"Bloody ketchup is good," said Eudora. "So where's Barney now?"

"That's just what *I* want to know," Brewer said, with an odd edge to his voice. He looked again down at Ann Laird and looked away. "I'm in the dark."

As though on cue, light streamed into the room—the outer door opened. Barney Noble ambled in, his good-natured eyes on Brewer's face. "Well, how did it go?"

Professor Brewer looked at him for a long moment. "Where have you been?" The question sounded slow and deadly.

The smile on Barney's face was a little uncertain. "Now don't get sore. I was late this morning, and when I opened the door I saw Ann and tumbled to the fact that the show was going on without me. Then Puccini yelled to me to clock him around the track, and that's what I've been doin'. I didn't see much point to showin' up in class. I knew all the answers."

Puccini, his long runner's legs pounding around the oval track that circled the green practice field. Barney watching him, watch in hand. And Ann Laird, dead behind a closed door, where Barney should have lain.

Brewer was looking at Barney, and his voice was still quiet and slow. "Did you speak to her?" he asked.

"Sure. I said, 'Hi, Toots.'" A delayed reaction took place on Barney's ruddy face. A look of uneasiness changed swiftly to puzzlement, and then to baffled, desperate horror. He whirled around and went quickly to Ann Laird's side. He stood there, looking down. Then he looked over at Brewer and Eudora. His face had lost most of its color. "She's dead."

Brewer nodded. There was silence for a moment. "Didn't it strike you as odd when she didn't answer you?" Brewer asked Barney at last.

Barney shook his head. "You see, she didn't like to be called Toots."

Brewer turned to Eudora. "Did you speak to her?"

"Yes."

"But you weren't surprised when she didn't answer?"

"No."

"I don't suppose that you, too, happened to call her Toots?" Brewer's voice was speeding up; some of his old assurance had returned.

"No."

"What did you say to her?"

Eudora tried to keep her voice steady. "I said, 'It seems that I did you in.' She didn't answer so I said, 'O.K., Ann. Don't take any wooden lilies.' "

Brewer gave her one long look and then lowered his eyes, saying abruptly, "I have to talk to President Trinklehaus about this. And phone the police—I believe that's customary in cases of accident. Don't spread the news around, you two. They may want to talk to you. I'll send for you if they do. How about that key I gave you, Noble?"

Barney fished down into the pocket of his cords. As he handed the key to Brewer he said, "The door wasn't locked. It was closed, but not locked."

"Well," said Eudora, with a last look at Ann Laird. She turned her eyes away.

"Well . . . ," said Barney, and scratched his crew haircut fiercely. Giving a quick look at Ann, he suddenly turned and bolted out the other door, slamming it after him. Brewer went over and locked it.

Eudora walked thoughtfully toward the inner door by which she and Brewer had entered. She was halfway down the lower corridor when Brewer fell into step beside her.

"She's been dead for some time," said Brewer.

"Yes. The blood was dry."

They had reached the foot of the stairs. Brewer switched out the lights, leaving the basement in darkness. They went up quickly, side by side. Eudora stopped thinking of the last time she had seen Ann alive, to wonder what Brewer was thinking. She cast a quick glance at him. He was frowning down at his feet, one hand rubbing his pointed chin. He left her at the first floor to continue to the second floor, where his office was. Eudora walked out onto the porch of Old College, and then her feet slowed and she stood silently in front of the bulletin board, looking into the uncannily alive eyes of a photograph: ANN LAIRD printed below it, and printed above it, JULIET.

Involuntarily she stood looking at the other photographs. ROMEO—*Paul Ober*: a handsome face, large eyes looking at nothing, on the mouth a small smile. MERCUTIO —*Oliver Clarey*: a tense face, a lean face, beard showing under the skin. FRIAR LAURENCE—*Dave Draska:* a thin face, long bright black eyes. She dropped her eyes to the flourishing script at the bottom of the poster: *Student Director—Dave Draska."* She turned away.

She walked across the street to the Wagon Wheel. It was Chapel Hour, so the booths were full and the juke box was going full blast. She sat at the counter and put her hands over her ears. "Coke," she said to the boy behind the counter, and tried to hunt down the thought that bothered her, like walking into a dark room and hearing someone stop breathing and stand very still.

She sipped her coke, and her mind went to dress rehearsal the night before. She felt again her hand pushing against the wood and the door opening, and again Brewer, standing just within, stepped aside to let her pass. She saw again above the heads of the scattering of spectators the bright glare of the stage, and heard again Ann's voice saying to the nurse, "What is yon gentleman? Go ask his name. . . . If he be married, my grave is like to be my wedding bed!"

Then Professor Romaine's unforgettable voice, resonant as bells, powerful as great music: "Juliet! More stars in your eyes! More stars in your voice!"

Romaine's voice! It had something to do with Romaine's voice, this shadow hiding in her mind. *Let's see,*

I went down the aisle. Millicent grabbed at my skirt and her glasses were gleaming in the light from the stage, and next to her Jim Laird was biting a fingernail, his eyes locked to Ann. Then I went up the side steps of the stage and into the wings, where Joe was looking for Juliet's dagger. And I was backstage when Romaine's voice said what I'm trying to remember.

Ah. The vial scene. Ann beside her couch, the vial raised aloft. Funny from the wings, because looking past her you saw faces looking out from the opposite wing, and someone scratching his ear. Ann's voice: "Romeo, I come! This do I drink to thee." And then Romaine's whisper saying, "That vial's too big." And aloud: "That sleeping potion—mysterious stuff. Potent. Strange. And Dave, you're having her toss off half a cup of it." Dave striding from the opposite wing then, his gray friar's robe billowing around his ankles. "You're right. Professor Romaine. Absolutely. What do you suggest?" And Romaine's voice: "Something small. Something glittering." And Ann Laird stepping forward to Dave's side, squinting past the foots, her voice eager: "There's a little silver vial down in the prop room. I'll get it right after rehearsal's over." And Romaine's voice: "Good."

Good.

Chapter Five: AND JULIET BLEEDING

AN HOUR later, in response to a message whispered by the secretary from the Sociology Office to the professor of her Social Psychology class, and relayed by him to her in a tone which suggested that she keep her dates and classwork from conflicting, Eudora knocked at the door of the prop room. It was opened by Professor Brewer, who at once retired to an army cot at the far end of the room, struck a match on the adjacent Chinese screen and drew closer a large brass vase. The match dropped into it with a faint bonging sound.

And then Eudora was dazed by the sight of a giant with seal-brown hair and a size 46 beige sport coat, standing beside the dark stain spread out beneath Ann Laird's head, making notes in a small black book with a pencil which was just two inches long.

"This is Miss York," called Brewer. "The student who found the body. Miss York, Lieutenant Tuck."

The giant looked at Eudora. His skin was the color of a well-smoked meerschaum pipe, his eyes the color of black coffee, and his long face was as expressionless as a statue. "How do you do?" he asked politely. His voice was not so deep as she had expected from his size, but if he stood on any stage and whispered, she knew she would hear him in the back row.

"Very well," she replied. "And you?"

I'm being sassy, she thought. *But he's so big!*

Tuck pointed down with the stubby yellow pencil. "How did you overlook the fact that she was dead?" he asked, almost politely. "She looks very dead to me."

"You have a basis for comparison," Eudora said. "I don't. This is the first dead body I've ever seen. To me she looked exactly like Ann Laird, with white powder on, acting a dead body."

"Some actress," said a sad voice, and a round, drooping face, topped by a black hat, peered out from behind Tuck and stared at her.

"This is Detective Froody," said Tuck.

" 'Do," said Froody, and became again invisible to her.

"The body was lying just this way when you saw it?" asked Tuck.

Eudora looked at Ann Laird. Certain details which she had not consciously noticed became apparent to her. Ann was lying on her back, one arm thrown out, the other at her side. Just beyond her head was a round, dark object which was part of the mental image Eudora had retained from her first glimpse of the body, but which she had not identified until this moment. It was one end of a bar-bell—a six-inch globe of dull black iron, the long iron bar and the other globe hidden below the large tin-topped table beside which Ann Laird was lying. A cast-away prop from some forgotten play.

"Yes," she said. "The body was like that."

Brewer dropped another match into the vase.

Tuck turned briskly to Professor Brewer. "This girl's death, of course, had no connection with the experiment you planned." He pointed down at the body. "X," he said, "marks the spot where two paths crossed. A path leading to a make-believe death, as you have explained, and another path, leading to an actual death, to the death of this young woman. She was dead a good many hours before either Mr. Noble or Miss York saw her. Which brings us to an odd question. What in the name of heaven was this girl doing in this prop room late last night?"

᾽ "I know," Eudora said calmly, and caused a little stir.

Froody peered at her again from just beyond Tuck's shielding bulk, and she heard the springs of the cot squeak as Brewer made a sudden movement.

Only Tuck remained impassive. "You do?" he said.

"Are you familiar with *Romeo and Juliet?*" she asked Tuck.

"I have a nodding acquaintance with it." He gave a brief smile which showed handsome white teeth.

"She was Juliet. The dress rehearsal was last night, and the faculty director decided that the vial she was using for the sleeping-potion scene was too big. Ann remembered a small silver vial among the hand props, and said that she would come down here for it. Rehearsal ended at five minutes to eleven. Allowing half an hour for her to get her make-up and costume off, she would have been down here looking for it at about eleven-thirty."

"Fine," Tuck said, exactly as though he were a professor and she had completed a superior recitation.

"She didn't get it," said Froody. "It isn't in her purse." And he extended the green suede purse which he had been clutching all the while he stood there.

"She might have had it in her hand when she fell," Tuck said. "It would have been flung wide as she felt herself falling, and might have landed anywhere. Froody, give a look around on the floor, dark corners and all."

"I think I can suggest a short-cut," said Eudora, and again everyone looked at her. She pointed up at a fruit box which stood, among other odds and ends, on a high shelf along the wall from which the big tin-topped table jutted. "It should be in that box of hand props."

Tuck's face didn't change, but something behind his eyes frowned. When he spoke, his words seemed to come out on tiptoes. "Professor Brewer tells me you're a Psychology major," he said.

"I am." She grinned up at him. "But there's something corny deep down inside me that loves grease paint and amber lights. So I'm also a Drama minor. I'm the biggest ham in the whole darned department, and that's saying a lot."

Unexpectedly, it was Professor Brewer who laughed. When she looked over at him, now standing before the cot, he explained, "I've been puzzled about that 'dead for a ducat.'" He smiled at her quite pleasantly, but she didn't like him any better than she ever had.

When she looked back at Tuck, he was standing on the tin-topped table, and a small flashlight was shedding its beam into the fruit box. He reached around with his free hand, pulled a handkerchief from his hip pocket, lapped it about his fingers and reached into the box. In a moment he turned, towering gigantically above them, and pointed the flashlight beam at a small, glittering silver vial he was holding delicately by the cap.

"That's it," said Eudora.

Tuck took a white envelope from his breast pocket, dropped the vial into it, licked the flap, sealed it, and put it away in his inner breast pocket. Then he took one huge step to the floor, jarring the room as he landed, and looked from the box to the slippery tin top of the table to Ann Laird's two-inch heels.

Boldly, Eudora asked, "Do you think she slipped?"

Before Tuck could answer, Brewer came forward and stood beside Eudora. He mopped his eternal flush and said, "I don't want to intrude my opinion, but there are a few things I'd like to mention. . . ."

"Please do," Tuck urged politely.

Froody came a little closer, and Brewer, with something of his classroom manner, pointed to the edge of the table and then to the wooden fruit box directly above it. "You will notice that in order to reach the box she would have had to stand on the extreme edge of the table. Tin is slippery. She has on very high heels. Furthermore, she isn't much over five feet three, and she would certainly have had to stand on tiptoe in order to look over the edge of the box."

"Right," Tuck said.

Brewer shrugged. "She made a false step, that's all. Down she went, struck her head on that iron weight, and the force of the blow killed her."

"Yes," agreed Tuck. "It could have happened that way. But it didn't."

They all looked up at him. As though embarrassed by that multiple stare, he started to walk toward the closed door to the practice field. Eudora had the sudden crazy notion that he would open it and walk quietly out of the room, leaving them to puzzle over what he had just said.

"You have some other theory?" Brewer asked.

Tuck turned his back to the door and looked at them across the room. "If you, Miss York, and Mr. Noble have both told me the exact truth, nothing more or less, someone else was in this room with this dead girl. Before Noble saw her body. Before you saw it, Miss York. And since this person did not report to the police that he had seen the body, I assume he had a very good reason—the reason being that he had killed her."

He half-turned, made a quick motion, and sudden bright light made Eudora blink. She opened her eyes to see the two electric bulbs which dangled from the ceiling nakedly aglow. Tuck unwrapped the white handkerchief from his hand and pointed with a long forefinger at the switch beside the door.

"Exactly," said Tuck. "Someone turned out the light." He added, "And it wasn't Ann Laird."

Chapter Six: THOUGHTS UTTERED

"AND NOW," Tuck said, "I'll have to phone headquarters. Fingerprint boys and photographers."

"There's a phone in the Psychology Office," offered Brewer.

"Thanks. I'm going to have some coffee, and I'll use a booth. Miss York, where's the nearest cup of coffee?"

"Across the street at the Wagon Wheel."

"You stay here," Tuck said to Froody. "The Doc should be here soon. Get down what he says and try to force him to be as definite as possible about the time."

"Don't let anyone in," Brewer warned Froody. "If this gets around before I've told President Trinklehaus, I'm cooked. And he won't be available for half an hour."

Froody lifted his lip, like a small fat mouse sneering. "What do you want I should do if someone opens a door, kick him in the face?"

"Give him those keys of yours," suggested Tuck to Brewer. "He can lock himself in." As Brewer handed Froody the two keys, Tuck said, "You're quite certain, Professor Brewer, there are only three keys to this room?

One to the inner door and two to the outer?"

"That's what the Drama School secretary told me."

As Brewer started out the inner door, Tuck and Eudora went out the other, into hot dazzling sunlight.

Tuck paused and then went over to a towering elm tree some 20 feet away. On the other side of the tree was a long green bench, its back to the door of the prop room. He squatted and removed another white envelope from his pocket. Eudora went swiftly to his side and stood looking down at five close-smoked cigarette ends lying in the grass. He picked them up, examined them one by one, and dropped them into the envelope.

"My," said Eudora. "I didn't dream that real detectives ever found cigarette butts."

"Oh, yes." He licked the envelope and put it away.

"What do you deduce from them?"

Tuck looked down at her. "Not much. They were dropped there before this morning's dew fell, and were probably all smoked by the same person. They're all Luckies."

"What kind of person?"

"I haven't the slightest idea."

"You can't even tell whether it was a man or a woman?"

"If it was a woman, she had no lipstick on."

"Then it was probably a man."

"Probably, but not necessarily."

"Waiting for someone!"

"Maybe. Maybe not. How about that coffee?"

"How," asked Eudora, as they walked across warm grass to the front of Old College, "can you be sure that the light was ever turned on?"

"The switch is just beside the only door she could have entered by. I'm not wrong in assuming that she would have known the switch was there, am I?"

"No."

"Well, she hadn't found the vial she was looking for,

so the light would still have been on when she was killed."

Eudora said, "There are several not too far-fetched reasons why someone might have found the body before either Barney or I did, and been averse to telling the police. That person could have turned the light off and yet still not be a murderer."

"You get to the point nicely," Tuck said, in a pleased voice. "If she wasn't murdered, she fell."

"Yes."

"I can't reconcile a fall with the fact that the back of her skull was bashed in."

"Oh," said Eudora. "I didn't know."

"Force was behind the blow that killed her," Tuck said. "I'm sure of that. And her body was moved after she fell."

"That," said Eudora, "makes it all very interesting."

"Have a cup of coffee with me," Tuck suggested. "You can tell me all about it."

Since the eleven-o'clock classes were still in session, all but one of the Wagon Wheel's knotty-pine booths were empty. A Freshman with muscular arms was polishing glasses behind the knotty-pine counter. Tuck asked her to order coffee and crammed himself into the knotty-pine phone booth.

Eudora had just taken her first sip of coffee when Tuck came back and by some miracle of muscular contraction squeezed into the bench opposite hers. She realized that her first impression had been correct: his eyes were exactly the color of black coffee. He took a gulp that emptied his cup by half, and then drew from his side coat pocket the small black notebook in which he had been writing when she first saw him in the prop room. She noticed again the stubbiness of his yellow pencil.

Tuck licked the pencil and poised it in readiness on the top line of a blank page. "Who loved her? Who hated her? Who knew her best?"

"I have some theories about the first two questions, but

I know the facts about the last."

"Facts first," Tuck commanded.

"Her husband knew her best. His name is Jim Laird."

While Tuck wrote he said, "Married, huh? How long?"

"A year, or a little more."

"Were they happy?"

"I never asked them."

"I'll reword my question. Did they seem happy?"

"Yes. Whenever I saw them."

"You didn't see them often?"

"No. I suspect they'd worked out some civilized arrangement about their friends, because Ann usually came to the Drama get-togethers without him. Jim didn't care too much for us. Once I saw him looking at Oliver Clarey as though at a toad when Oliver was reciting poetry over his beer. Jim is a successful commercial artist. He's very practical. He's not 'arty.' "

"Were they in love?" Tuck asked.

"In love?"

"That's rather important. I should say that it's more important in a marriage than money."

"Mr. Tuck," said Eudora, "you astound me. Very well. I believe they were rather more in love than the average young couple. It was a love tempered on both sides by desire for personal success. Ann's talent came first with Ann—she could no more help that than she could help breathing. I think she was lucky to have married an artist, who would be able to understand that, being a little the same way himself."

"What sort of a person is he—besides being a good commercial artist, I mean?"

"I've never seen them apart, so what I say about him includes Ann—and maybe it throws a bit more light on their marriage. I remember them walking down campus together. I think they were going here for dinner. Ann had just got the part of Juliet, and she was in heaven. I saw them coming toward me, a tall blond man with a mild strong face, taking mild, long strides—and a small dark thing with her eyes shining, tugging at his arm and talking up at him very fast. And then, a week or so after that, when Ann was depressed about the voting scandal—"

"The voting scandal?" said Tuck.

"Oh, yes. Whenever Play Productions is casting for a new show, the student director and the faculty director decide on several possible castees for each important part. The members of Play Productions vote on those nominees —by closed ballot. There were two nominees for the part of Juliet—Ann and Meg Fife. The winner would play on opening night, the loser would take two of the three following and less important performances. Ann won by one vote—and a rumor began circulating that she voted for herself."

"Why not?" asked Tuck.

"Well, a hypocritical notion has been current in the group for years that you never vote for yourself. Ann was crushed, and I think I know why. I'm sure she didn't vote for herself, and I think what smashed her was the realization that someone hated her enough to start such a story."

"This all had some point a few minutes ago. Let's go back."

"Oh. Well, I saw Jim and Ann walking along University again, the night this came out. This time Ann was walking very slowly, hunched over with her hands jammed in the pockets of her polo coat. Her sparkle was gone—she wasn't even pretty. She was completely a different person from the other Ann. And Jim Laird was leaning down toward her, talking to her in that quiet voice of his, and for an instant it struck me that a stranger would take them for brother and sister."

Tuck said, "I like your way of telling what you know. I can see you don't have much respect for hearsay evidence. Everything you've told me about these two people has been either plainly labeled as a judgment of your own, or has been a concrete description."

"Thanks," said Eudora. She had never been so pleased at a compliment.

"Who do you think started the story that Ann voted for herself?"

"I don't know," said Eudora slowly. "I'm sorry I don't, because I have the notion that it's very important."

"Who's Meg Fife?"

"Restrained. One of those clear, fine voices, with a New York accent. She's small—smaller even that Ann. But she has big feet. *Very* big feet. And her ankles escape being thick by a sixteenth of an inch."

"Why don't you like her?" smiled Tuck.

"She's too conscious of her own superiority. She imposes a high standard of conduct upon herself and wears it instead of jewelry."

Tuck grinned. "I've noticed one thing a woman hates more than a bad woman—a very good one."

"Don't be witty," Eudora said. "Dave Draska has exactly my feelings about Meg, only more so. He says that only some dark deed in her past could justify constant care to present such eternal fineness to the world."

"Ah-ha," said Tuck, and jotted three words beside Meg's name. Eudora strained, read it upside down, and was a little amazed to see: *Bag or bustle.*"

"How about this Dave Draska?" Tuck asked.

"He's a tall, skinny, catty Russian. There's a story which, if true, will tell you more about him than anything I might say. Last September, at the start of Registration Week, a car a block long drove up in front of the Administration Building. Dave was standing on the porch. I am told he said, 'If the person at the wheel of that car is a man, he's going to become my closest friend. If it's a woman, I'm going to marry her.' It was a woman, plump rich girl named Lily Forbes, and they are now engaged."

"Which doesn't prove the story is true," put in Tuck.

"Does that really matter? The point is, it seems to me, that Dave Draska is the sort of person about whom such a story could be told and be believed."

"All this seems pretty innocuous," Tuck complained. "Didn't anyone hate her guts?"

"Yes. The person who spread the story that she voted for herself."

Tuck sighed. "And I suppose there's no hope of a Romeo, other than the husband?"

"I think not. I room with her closest friend, to whom Ann used to make certain confidences, and who absolutely trembled all over every time she mentioned how crazy Ann was about Jim. A woman having an affair would inevitably talk about her lover to her closest friend. If she was smart enough to keep her mouth shut about him, she would certainly not get dewy-eyed about the husband."

"A woman of the world, that's what you are."

"I know a little about people," said Eudora coldly. "That just takes being alive for twenty-two years and keeping your eyes open."

"I'm squashed," Tuck said. "So no affair. So she was hated by a Miss or Mr. X, loved by her husband and her best friend. This is very dull."

"She was loved by someone else, too," Eudora said slowly. "A boy named Oliver Clarey. He's been in love with her for three years."

"Tell me about him."

"I don't like Oliver. He acts, on stage and off. He even dramatizes his feeling for Ann, not that that minimizes it in the least. He's loudly cheerful, desperately gay, with one of those big voices that never change pitch. He and Ann met when she was a Junior and he a Sophomore. He's a Senior now. She's—she was taking her M.A. in Dramatics. I didn't know either of them then, but I used to see them striding together along campus, taking the same length steps, with the wind blowing her hair around. They were always laughing. Once, I remember, they went past me singing, 'A capital ship for an ocean trip was the walloping Window Blind.' I thought it was the epitome of gay young love. Ann couldn't carry a tune—her sincere enjoyment of music must have been based on vibrations she got through the soles of her feet. So there they went singing, Oliver in his big baritone, Ann piping away, blissfully off-key, and neither of them noticing."

"You've convinced me," Tuck said. "He loves her."

"Who loves who?" demanded an easy voice, from just behind Eudora's right shoulder.

She looked up into Paul Ober's face, looking down at her with that small smile which didn't suit the melancholy, sea-colored eyes. He slipped into the booth beside Eudora with casual ease, began to play with a spoon with his thin brown fingers, looked straight into her eyes, still smiling, and asked, "Have you see Ann around?"

Tuck leaned forward. "I'm Richard Tuck."

Paul gave him a lazy look. "Paul Ober," he said, and reached a hand across the table with a gesture which seemed slow but wasn't. The two men shook hands.

Tuck caught Eudora's eye.

"We've got to go, Paul," she said, and stood up.

Paul also rose and stood aside to let her squeeze from the booth. She smiled at Paul and caught him looking at Tuck. Tuck was also standing, and next to him Paul looked like a child—a tan-throated child in a navy-blue sweater. For just an instant his eyes traveled up Tuck's height, and Eudora knew he was thinking that three of Tuck's inches would very probably make the difference between the success or failure of his own life. Paul had one of the handsomest faces Eudora had ever seen, a muscular coordination that made his every motion on stage an unconscious masterpiece of timing, one of those voices that take

any line and make it unforgettable. And he was exactly
five feet five inches tall.

"Are you one of these single-standard chaps, or are you
going to pay for my coffee?" she asked Tuck, too brightly
and too loudly.

"When Tuck treats, he treats!" Tuck replied.

Paul Ober smiled. They left him sitting alone.

"Who's he?" asked Tuck, on University Avenue.

"Romeo."

"In the play?"

"In the play."

"Where can I find Jim Laird? For some hours it has been
high time for the anxious young husband to have appeared, making inquiries as to the whereabouts of his
young wife who didn't come home last night. So where can
I find him?" Tuck asked patiently.

"All I know is he works at a large advertising agency
downtown. The person you want to see is my roommate,
Millicent Legg."

"And where can I find Millicent Legg?"

"She's in class now. I think in the Administration Building." She pointed out the big, square-towered, red-brick
building, a block ahead of them on the same side of University Avenue as Old College. "What you'd better do is
go into the Student Union book store—the Student Union's
that square atrocity just across the side-street from the
Administration Building. On a long table beside the door
are some narrow boxes full of section cards. And section
cards are full of the names, addresses, phone numbers and
class schedules of every student on campus."

They crossed University and stopped face-to-face with
Professor Brewer.

"I've talked with President Trinklehaus," he informed
them. "He took it very well. So now, Miss York, you're
relieved of the strain of holding your tongue, if you have
held it. I know that's always hard on a woman." He

grinned and passed on toward Old College.

Eudora looked up at Tuck. "Grrrr," she said.

Tuck grinned and left her. He found the number of the room where Millicent Legg was attending a lecture that hour; then he found the room and went in. The professor suspended his lecture and cocked his head in strained politeness while Tuck explained that it was of utmost importance that he speak to Miss Legg.

Miss Legg turned out to be a very small young woman who rose in great confusion, gathered, with the aid of the student each side, an enormous stack of books, trotted beside Tuck to the empty corridor outside the classroom. There she peered up at him through thick glasses. "Yes?" she asked, in a high and childishly puzzled voice.

"I'm Lieutenant Tuck, of the Los Angeles Homicide Squad," Tuck began without preface.

"Homicide Squad?" shrilled Millicent Legg. The eyes got wider, unbearably wider.

Tuck made his voice calm, very professional. "Your friend Ann Laird is dead, Miss Legg."

Millicent Legg held his eyes with hers for a short minute, moaned and fainted. Tuck methodically stacked her scattered books, raised the lower part of her tiny body with them, dampened his big white handkerchief at a near-by drinking fountain, laid it on her forehead, and waited for the blood to return to the pinched white face and the blank brain behind it.

Chapter Seven: WHAT HAVE WE HERE?

EUDORA SAT in the small office on the first floor of Old College beside the desk that belonged to Professor Romaine. The first time she ever saw the desk, she knew it was Professor Romaine's—it was unbelievably crowded, and with such an odd assortment of objects. A lovely little cloisonné vase containing one incredibly perfect unfolding rose. A towering stack of students' papers, which Professor Romaine assigned with mad abandon, and, so rumor had it, never read, unless she happened to be very fond of the student. A pair of bookends were alabaster doves, between them one slim book—*The Ballad of Reading Gaol*. Beside the book-ends, a stack of paper-bound playscripts. In the center of the green blotting pad one of these was in the process of being cut. Cut literally, with a pair of large shears.

Suddenly Eudora's eyes stopped on the topmost of the students' papers. Like the others, it was bound in the conventional bookstore folder of shiny tan manila, and on the front was a printed box containing the student's name, the date, and the name of the class. This one said: "*Ann Laird, Advanced Drama II, June 9.*" Yesterday, the day she died.

She stood up, went to the desk, and began to read:

You have asked me, Professor Romaine, for a paper on the character of Juliet. If I had time to be studious about this, I would include some remarks about Shakespeare's women, and some impressive comments on great portrayals of the Juliet character. But I haven't time. Not only must I go over the balcony scene with Paul Ober in an hour and half, but there are some annoying dishes awaiting my magic touch in the kitchen sink, and as I type this I can look straight into the faces of three dying roses which should have been decently cremated in the incinerator at least two days ago.

So this is all I have to say. An actress who plays Juliet as sweetly pitiful is underscoring unnecessarily what is implicit in the story the play tells. Juliet should be played as a headlong and fiery child—never cloying, always conscious of love burning within her body. She never grows up, not even with the final words, "O happy dagger! This is thy sheath. There rust and let me die!" For even as she stabs herself, she is still the child, undisillusioned by life's small tricks, and so able to make the terrible and right decision without thought of compromise.

As for the lovers, the beauty and irony of their tragedy lies in the fact that their two names connote for all the world the high brave final degree of young love only because they died young. If they had lived—

A sound made Eudora turn, a little guiltily. Professor Romaine was entering the office. She always entered a room sideways, the tall body gracefully following the tailored, leading shoulder; and she always electrified any room, anywhere, any time.

Today there was a flush on the thin ivory cheeks, accented by gray hair that as usual escaped the bondage of her smart brown mannish hat. Below the brim of the hat the huge brown eyes were blazing.

Eudora said, "You told me yesterday you had a part you wanted me to do for the class."

Professor Romaine nodded her head wisely. Her lips with their splash of careless crimson pursed, but it was not quite a smile. "I have," she said in her deep voice, and glided to the bookcase beside her desk. She tweaked a volume of plays from one of its jumbled rows, opened it to the place she wanted with a quick slash of one long thin hand, and suddenly held the open book out at arm's length, a foot away from Eudora's astonished eyes.

"*The Vultures!*" she proclaimed. "Choose any scene. I am sure you could do all of them equally well!" She thrust the book into Eudora's nerveless hands, closed her eyes, and turned her back.

Eudora surmised that the interview was over and went numbly out of the office. *She's angry at me*, she was thinking. *She's angry at me, and because I was reading Ann Laird's last paper. That's it! She was calling me a vulture.* A new thought struck her. *But how*, she wondered, with a hot flash of alarm somewhere near her stomach, *does she know Ann is dead?* . . .

Brewer was in the act of leaving his office for lunch. He was a trifle annoyed at the delay. "No, I haven't told anyone but President Trinklehaus. Why should I?"

Walking down the stairs, and along the first-floor corridor in which a few delayed and luncheon-bound students were hurrying, she thought, *That leaves Barney
Noble, which is very odd, because I doubt whether he's
ever spoken to Professor Romaine.*

Dave Draska was sitting on the rough stucco wall of the
porch, his back against the pillar that helped form the
arch at the head of the steps, eating a chocolate bar with
delicate maneuverings of the protective wrapper. Hearing footsteps on the cement, he turned his head on its long
thin neck and looked at her out of narrow eyes.

"Where were you last night, darling?" he asked. "You
really missed a treat. We met at Carlo's Café, sat outside
under the umbrellas, and had a perfectly delightful time
telling each other how good we were."

"I had a headache."

He cocked his head in mock sympathy. "How too bad."
He dropped the bantering manner abruptly. "Seriously, I
think we have a darned fine show."

She nodded impatiently and started down the steps.

"I hope nothing happens," he called after her, and she
glanced up to see him watching her.

She found Barney Noble, as she had hoped to, in one of
the booths of the Wagon Wheel. He was eating a hot
beef sandwich with glum pleasure, and as he looked up at
her he licked a dab of gravy from the corner of his mouth.
The other two big lumpy men with crew haircuts and
lettermen's maroon sweaters went on eating.

"Listen, Barney," she said, standing at the end of the
table, "did you tell Professor Romaine about Ann?"

"Who's Professor Romaine?" asked Barney. "Anything
new? About Ann, I mean. Here, have a seat." He edged
closer to the wall, and she sat down.

"You didn't tell Romaine about Ann. Brewer says he
didn't. I didn't. But she knows, Barney. Who told her?"

"It must have been Draska. I ran into him just after I left the prop room this morning. Gosh, I hardly know the bird, and I spouted like a geyser." He made a path across a mound of mashed potato with the tines of his fork. "It seemed like I just had to tell someone."

"What's cooking, cookie?" one of the athletes asked Eudora.

She said, "Don't you think of anything but food?" and stood up.

"Ann Laird's dead," said Barney Noble. Something in his voice made Eudora listen. The voice was trying to be unmoved, and was not quite succeeding.

"Who's Ann Laird?" asked the other athlete. "Do I know her?"

Barney looked down at his plate. In spite of his size, he was a small boy not wanting any more dinner. He pushed the plate slowly away from him. "She was Juliet," he said.

She crossed University Avenue with her eyes on Dave Draska, still perched on the wall. As she flew up the steps she decided a blunt approach was best. "Did you tell Professor Romaine that Ann is dead?" she asked.

He nodded and crumpled the wrapper of his candy bar, tossing it down into the bushes below.

"When?"

"Just at the start of lunch hour. She was beating her way to her office and I stopped her and told her. I'm calling a special meeting of Play Productions in order to decide what's to be done about the show."

She swung to the wall beside him. "Why didn't you tell me that you knew, just now?"

"I wanted to ask a couple of questions first. You see, there were just two people noticeable by their absence last night at Carlo's. One was Ann and the other was you. You see, she could have been murdered."

"What possible motive would I have for murdering her?" Eudora asked.

Draska raised one shoulder in an elaborate shrug. "What motive could anyone have?" His actor's voice was low and gentle. "I shall always remember Ann as a bright comet—a girl dynamic with talent, changeable with many moods, but really kind and really generous." The voice altered. A new faucet was turned on, and from the tap ran a whisper, fearful and momentous: "Who would kill a person like Ann? There's something crazy here." He jumped down from the wall. "I have to start rounding people up for that meeting. Be there, will you? It's at two, in Touchstone."

At the head of the steps he stopped and walked slowly over to the bulletin board in the corner. He stood with his back to Eudora, looking at it, and then he whirled around, genuine excitement on his face. He beckoned swiftly. "Come here! I said there was something crazy at work—look at this!" He pointed to the glass-covered easel, and his long finger was an exclamation point.

Chapter Eight: THE WIDOWER

THROUGH THE glass partition that walled off the inner office, where five shirt-sleeved artists were bent in silent absorption over their battle-scarred drawing boards, Tuck had seen a man who fitted the description of Jim Laird which Eudora York had given him an hour before. He smiled confidently at the secretary and went to the man's side.

Jim Laird's hands were not the popular conception of what an artist's hands should look like. They were spare hands, not very large, with spatulate fingers that worked as deftly as a surgeon's. But the closely bitten nails wore the dinge of India ink, and a splash of red paint across the back of the right hand, shaped like a scar, plastered down the fine blond hairs against the fair skin.

"Mr. Laird?" asked Tuck.

The blond man looked up. An arc of straight tan hair

hung down over the wide forehead, which, with the corn-silk eyebrows and sandy lashes, gave the face a boyish look. But the square strong chin and firmness of the square underlip offset this. So did the voice.

It was a mild and dignified voice. "Yes."

"Mr. Laird, I want to speak to you for a few minutes, and I think it had better be alone."

The pale blue eyes widened a trifle. The pleasant voice was undisturbed. "I'm pretty busy right now."

"It's important," Tuck said.

Jim looked through the glass that separated the work-room from the outer office. "The secretary's leaving for lunch. We can talk out there. Just a minute."

He turned back to his drawing board, dipped a fine brush into a jar of white paint, and with one long sure stroke made perfect the slightly blurry edge of a big script "C." Reluctantly, his eyes still on his work, Jim Laird stood up, swished the brush in a jelly jar of gray water, and automatically combed back his hair.

"O.K." He led the way to the outer office, half-sat on the secretary's desk and pulled out a pipe, which he filled from an oiled-silk pouch. "What's the deal?" he asked, and struck a match on the sole of a tan shoe.

"Your wife's dead, Mr. Laird. She's been murdered."

Jim Laird froze in the act of lighting his pipe. The match burned, the flame grew smaller and seared Laird's fingers. With a jerk he snapped it to the floor. He lowered the pipe from his mouth, and the hand that held it trembled. The faintly ruddy face had gone white, and the pupils of the light eyes had dilated. Tuck knew, on the basis of many years' experience, that this shock was real. Jim tried to speak and then shook his head.

"I was called to the University this morning at ten by the head of the Psychology Department. Her body had been found by a Psychology student at nine-thirty in the prop room. She had been dead for some hours, killed by a blow on the head."

"No," Laird whispered, "she couldn't have been. She was in bed, asleep, when I left for work this morning."

"You mean, you saw her in bed and asleep?"

Laird shook his head dully. "No. The door was shut. But—" He looked down at the unlighted pipe still held loosely in his limp right hand. Then he stood up slowly, turned his back to Tuck and walked three steps away. He stood there quite still for a full minute, and then turned. "Take me to her," he commanded. His voice was like a body drained of blood.

"It's not necessary," said Tuck. "She's at the city morgue. You will be asked to identify her at the coroner's inquest, but it could do no good to see her now."

"How—?" began Jim Laird, and then the voice stopped, and the hand with the crimson splash of paint went slowly to the forehead and stayed there.

"May we go to your home now?" Tuck asked. "I'm going to have to pry a little. That's my job."

Tuck in his black sedan followed Laird's open black convertible with its bright-red leather upholstery across the glaring noonday heat of the city of Los Angeles. Jim Laird drove like an automaton; twice he missed collision with other cars by a last-minute twist of the wheel. A few blocks from the campus, Laird came to a stop in front of a new white rambling apartment house, built around a patio where pink hibiscus spread wide cups in the sun.

Tuck parked in back of Jim's car and followed him along the walk to a flight of steps leading to a balcony with a white iron railing. Jim grated a key into a white door and pushed it aside, waiting with automatic politeness for Tuck to enter.

On a maple coffee-table was a small blue vase from which drooped three dying red roses. Also an ashtray overflowing with cigarette butts—and a battered folder that looked like the script of a play. The studio couch had been opened out for use as a bed, and a welter of sheets and blankets was flung back over its foot.

Laird walked the length of the room and turned into a little hallway. Tuck followed, and when Jim opened the closed door at the end of the hall looked over his shoulder at a double bed which had not been slept in.

Tuck turned and went back into the living-room. Jim followed him slowly. The first impression of poor house-keeping was correct. The blue carpet had not been recently vacuumed. The furniture had not been recently dusted. Tuck stopped at the swinging door that led from the dining alcove into a small kitchen. On the drain-board of the sink, dishes were drying in a metal rack.

He turned back to the living-room and noticed the pic-tures—all good.

Jim Laird saw the direction of Tuck's look. "Ann framed those," he said. Laird seemed to be telling of something that had happened a long time ago.

Tuck looked at another picture. A gray day. Three sea gulls wheeling in the grayness. Beyond angry black rocks, the hull of an old sailing vessel, melting into the fog. It was a lonely scene, and good. He saw Laird's name in the corner. "That's nice," he said.

Laird looked at Tuck out of that hurt white face. "Thanks," he said, and sat down on a hard armchair.

Tuck sat opposite him in a big, flowered-chintz wing chair, beside the door that led to the little hallway and the neat, empty bedroom beyond.

Jim said, "You have to ask me questions. Ask 'em." He was looking at the blue carpet.

"I think I get the general drift," Tuck said. "But I'd like to hear from you how it happened that you didn't know that your wife didn't come home last night."

Laird raised his eyes from the rug to Tuck's face. Tuck noticed that already there were old shadows in the hol-lows below the boy's cheekbones. His lips were bloodless.

"I came home right after the dress rehearsal of her play was over. I mounted some sketches and went to bed." His eyes went to a desk and Tuck saw three neatly stacked watercolors. "I'd been sleeping in here for the last week," Jim went on. "The rehearsals kept Ann late, and we decided it would be better that way. I have to leave for work at eight in the morning. I forgot to set the alarm last night, and I didn't wake up until ten to eight, so I threw on my clothes and was out of the house in five minutes. That's why I didn't open the bedroom door."

"Do you know of any enemy your wife had?"

"No. Everyone liked Ann."

"Laird, I've been told that your wife was very much in love with you."

Jim Laird nodded. "Yes," he said simply.

"Was there anyone who loved her? Anyone who might have made an unwelcome advance and been a little too bluntly repulsed? And then lost his head?"

"A guy named Clarey made an ass of himself by wearing his heart on his sleeve. He and Ann went around for a while when they were undergraduates. I never took him very seriously. One of these dramatic guys."

"How did Mrs. Laird feel toward him?"

"She avoided him as much as possible."

"How about Paul Ober?"

Laird shook his head. "They were like a couple of men together."

"Any woman who might have been jealous of her?"

"No." Laird hesitated. "I don't think so."

"She must have been an unusual woman," said Tuck.

"She was."

Suddenly a telephone bell rang in the little apartment. Jim got up and went to the inner hall. A French phone was in a little niche in the wall opposite Tuck's chair. By twisting around, he saw Laird lift the phone from its cradle and put the receiver to his ear. He heard the soft

quack of a man's voice on the other end of the wire. Jim
stood for a moment, his back to Tuck, listening. Then he
dropped the phone into place and turned around. A new
look was on his face. Overlying the dead flatness of complete shock, held under control by a magnificent effort of
pride and will, was a new look—like the beginning of
horror."That was a man's voice. He said, 'Laird? Your
wife is dead, and I know who killed her.'"

"Yes," said Tuck. "I heard." He went to the phone and
dialed the operator. Laird moved into the living-room like
a person in a dream. "I want you to trace a call," said
Tuck to the operator's impersonal voice. "It was put
through to this number about three minutes ago. I'll
wait here. Phone when you get something. This is Lieutenant Tuck of the Homicide Squad."

He returned to the wing chair. Laird was sitting in the
stiff armchair opposite Tuck. He was staring at the carpet
again. Before either of them thought of anything to say,
the telephone bell pealed sharply. Tuck went to it.

"I cannot trace that call for you," said the operator, still
speaking in that far-away, plain voice. "It was placed
through dial equipment."

"Thank you," said Tuck. "No go," he said to Laird, and
started toward the front door.

Laird stood up as though pulled to his feet by strings.
"It was a nasty voice," he said slowly.

Chapter Nine: ONE THAT WAS A WOMAN

A WOMAN with gray hair showing wildly each side of her
hat was sitting at a littered desk, her back to the tall, old-
fashioned window that looked out over the athletic field
at the rear of Old College. Afternoon sunlight slitted
through the almost-closed Venetian blinds. A thin youth,
with a long neck and unctuous hair, was sitting on a
straight chair, leaning toward her. As Tuck opened the

door, he was saying, "...whatever you think best, of course, but—" He looked up at Tuck then and stopped talking. The tall woman at the desk waited for him to speak.

"Professor Romaine?" asked Tuck.

"Yes?" she said, making the word, like a deep voice coming up from a well, both a response and a question.

"I am Lieutenant Tuck. Professor Brewer told me you are in charge of the play whose leading lady has so unfortunately died. I have come to ask you to help me in the investigation of her death." He found that he was phrasing his words punctiliously, in deference to the regal quality of the woman before him.

"Professor Brewer," said Professor Romaine, "was in error. Mr. Draska," and she nodded toward the lean youth, "is in equal charge. He is the student director."

"Oh," said Tuck. "Well—"

"Please sit down," suggested Professor Romaine. "In what way can I help?"

Tuck sat down on a straight chair at one corner of her desk. "I want to question the students who were present at the dress rehearsal last night."

Professor Romaine said pleasantly, "That should take some time. There were about forty of them."

"Of whom some knew Mrs. Laird very well, and some scarcely at all," said Tuck.

"I am confused," stated Professor Romaine. "Mr. Draska has told me that this morning Ann was found in the prop room dead, that she had been apparently struck on the head. Do you think one of her friends did that?"

"I don't know," Tuck said.

"Ah," said Professor Romaine.

"What I do know is this. The person who killed her must have known she was going to the prop room after rehearsal was over. He must have either waited for her there or gone there to meet her. The chance that the person who had a reason for killing her happened to be in that room at such an unlikely hour is very far-fetched indeed."

"It was not an accident?"

"I think not."

Abstractedly Professor Romaine drew a cigarette from the big purse which lay on the desk. She lighted it, took one puff, inhaled deeply and exhaled a thin cloud of smoke. Then she dropped the cigarette to the floor and stepped on it. "I have never been more bewildered in my life," she said. "You know, of course, that at my suggestion the vial was changed?"

"Yes."

"So now you want me to tell you anything I know that might be relevant to this—" she paused; after a moment she went on, and her voice had fire in it—"this hideous thing."

"Yes."

"I can tell you absolutely nothing, Mr. Tuck."

Tuck nodded once. "I can understand, of course. Your relationship to the dead girl was confined to the classroom where she was one of many faces."

Professor Romaine closed her eyes and shook her head. "My students are not faces to me, Mr. Tuck. I have never had two students who were alike. I never expect to." Professor Romaine opened her eyes. They were sad. "Ann Laird had a soul," she said. "I was very fond of that soul." She stood up. "And now I am going home," she said. She waved one long hand at Draska. "Mr. Draska will make all the necessary arrangements."

Tuck rose. "Thank you so much—" he began.

Her huge eyes grew darker. "Oh, don't thank me," she said wearily. "I have done nothing. There is nothing I can do." She turned her eyes carefully sideways from his face and moved toward the door, following her own square shoulder. Abruptly she turned around. Suddenly her voice had a power in it like rivers rushing to the sea. "Look for a dark heart, Mr. Tuck!" she said. "Look for a sick mind! Look for madness!" Then she went.

"Well," said Draska. His eyes were still following Professor Romaine down the long corridor of Old College. He faced Tuck. "Well, I know just how she feels. Honestly, this thing is unbelievable." He drew himself a little taller. "I am entirely at your service, Mr. Tuck."

Tuck sat down. "I want to question everyone who knew her. Let's begin with you."

Draska looked surprised, and sat down too. "Well, I've known Ann for a year. We always got on very nicely. I'll be frank. We weren't exactly crazy over each other, but we got along. You know—"

"I know," said Tuck. "I had in mind something a bit more definite. For instance, when was the last time you saw her alive?"

"Just a few minutes after the last curtain. Lily—my fiancée—came backstage after the show and suggested that we have the usual get-together at Carlo's. I agreed and started to spread the news. I saw Ann in a huddle with the stage director and told her about it, and she said swell and asked me to tell her husband, if he was still out front. I did, and he declined, and then I went straight to the men's dressing-room. You have no idea, Mr. Tuck, how hot about five yards of monk's cloth can be."

"Where's the men's dressing-room?"

"I'll show you." Draska went to the door of the office, and Tuck followed. The doorway in which they were standing was at the junction of the main corridor and a rear corridor corresponding to the one in the basement which led to the prop room. Beside the door to Professor Romaine's office a staircase ascended to the second floor, forming a partial dead end to the main hallway. Tuck left Draska, went around to the side of that staircase and looked over an oaken handrail at the dark stairs leading down to the basement.

Draska came to his side. He pointed to a door directly opposite the balustrade over which Tuck had just peered. "That's the women's dressing-room," he said. "The men's is just above it, on the second floor." He walked to a spot in front of the door to Professor Romaine's office and Tuck followed.

Draska pointed down the main corridor to a wide double door in its right wall. "That door opens onto the central aisle of the theater." He then swung his arm in a quarter-circle and pointed far down the rear corridor to another double door in what Tuck judged to be the side wall of the theater. "That door," explained Draska, "leads into the wings. During a performance the prop staff puts up screens along here—" He turned and walked in a straight line across the end of the main corridor proper, and then back again to Tuck's side, "—so that the actors can go from the dressing-rooms and along this back hall to the door leading to the wings, and vice versa." He grinned. "Rather makeshift facilities, but when the trustees built this place in the '80's they intended Touchstone Theater to be used only as an auditorium where genteel song recitals might be given amid potted palms and restrained applause."

"Thank you," said Tuck. "You've made it quite clear." He looked down the length of the rear hall. "The stage, then, is above the prop room."

"Yes. Just about."

"But there's no staircase between them."

"No. You can get to the prop room only by these back stairs, or by going out the front of the building, around to the side, and through the outer door of the prop room."

"And after you went up to the men's dressing-room, you didn't see Ann Laird again?"

"No."

The door from the main hall to the theater opened, and

Paul Ober sauntered into the hall, saw them and walked toward them.

"I have something else to tell you, Mr. Tuck. Something to show you, I should say," Draska said quickly in a low tone, and to Paul, "Yes, my friend?"

"Everyone's here," said Ober. "They're getting mighty restless. I myself have a class in fifteen minutes, so it would be nice, my friend, if you got the lead out."

"Be right with you," said Draska loftily.

Ober gave Tuck a brief salute of recognition, turned as fluidly as a swimmer turning in water and started back toward the doors to the theater.

"I'll show you something in a little while that'll bowl you over," Draska said hurriedly.

"First," said Tuck, "I want to talk to the people who were in the theater last night."

Draska took his arm and led him down the rear hallway to the wings. "I think the best way to handle it would be for you to wait on stage while I make my announcement and get the voting over with."

"Voting?"

"Yes. When I asked Professor Romaine what to do about the show, she said the usual way, by ballot. We're a very democratic little organization. It should only take about five minutes. Then I'll have the students come backstage one by one, and you'll be able to question them privately."

They walked down the rear corridor, and Draska opened the door to the wings. Tuck looked onto a black stage, with one crack of light seeping in between the curtains, from beyond which came the multitudinous murmur of people waiting for something to happen.

Draska left Tuck standing in the doorway and went quickly and confidently to the opposite wing. In a moment four rows of red, white and blue bulbs were glaring down from overhead. Draska was standing before a panel full of switches and buttons in the front wall of the other wing. He turned, picked up a small wooden table and lugged it to stage center, where he dropped it with a thud.

"There. Grab that chair beside you and you're all set."

A monotonous clapping of hands began from beyond the curtain.

"O. K.?" asked Draska, one lean hand ready to push aside the curtain. "O. K.," said Tuck. Draska parted the curtains with a consciously dramatic gesture and stepped through.

Tuck sat down on a small folding chair before the small wooden table and looked about him. Instead of scenery, velvet curtains of a dark blue were being used, which gave the rather small stage a smothered, closed-in atmosphere. Both wings and, he guessed, the space in back of the encircling draperies were packed with necessary properties which would be lugged into place by the prop men after the fall of each curtain. *Rather the way the Old Boy himself must have staged it at the Globe Theater,* he thought. He became aware of Draska's well-modulated, artificial voice speaking to the audience:

"What I am going to tell you is so terrible and so unexpected that I can't believe it yet myself. I am going to ask you to control your grief as best you can and cooperate with me to the hilt. Here is the news I have for you. Ann Laird is dead."

There was utter silence for a long moment, and then, beginning with one or two incredulous voices, a babble of astonishment beat against the curtains.

"Please!" came Draska's voice imperiously. "Please!" Tuck could picture him holding both thin arms aloft on a command for silence. Slowly, reluctantly, the babble died to a murmur and at last ceased.

"As individuals," Draska went on, in a smooth voice, "our first concern is for Ann, whom we all loved and admired. But, as *troupers,* as members of a profession with a long tradition, our first concern is for the performance this evening, for which tickets have been sold and invitations mailed."

There was a dull silence.

"How did she die? What happened to her?" asked a voice with strain in it. And another, "What happened? She was all right last night!"

Draska's voice was crisp. "She may have been killed." He talked right through the tense murmur that arose. "I suggest that we vote at once on whether or not tonight's performance will go on. I should like to remind you that we are fortunate in having in Meg Fife a Juliet who has attended every rehearsal and who could step on stage tonight and play the part beautifully." A pause. "Would you be able to do it, Meg?" Draska called.

A woman's voice said so quietly that only excellent diction made it audible at all, "I don't know."

Draska went on, "As you all know, it has for many years been the policy of the Drama Department to invite to this show a number of influential people from the worlds of drama, radio and motion-pictures. Many students have received their start in this profession because someone who had the necessary influence saw them in this very theater and gave them a boost toward fame. I am wondering whether those influential people would be inclined to attend future performances if they arrived tonight, giving up their valuable time to do so, and were met with closed doors. Believe me, I am thinking now not of ourselves, but of all the later generations of young students who will come after us, to use these same dressing-rooms and walk these same boards in search of a future. As I say, we all knew and loved Ann Laird. I am wondering now what she would want us to decide."

Boy, thought Tuck, *you have the gift, all right. That was a neat bit of sentiment-swaying.*

"We will vote by closed ballot, as usual," Draska was saying. "Just tear a small piece of paper from your notebook and write on it 'yes,' meaning that the show will go on; 'no,' of course, the opposite."

A short silence; then ragged sounds of paper being torn. A girl's voice said, "I don't know *what* to do!"

After another silence Draska said, "Eudora, will you help me count the votes?"

The voice of the audience began again, not a babble this time, but a soft mutter, full of surmise, of bits of sentences. Somewhat closer to Tuck's ears, and after several minutes, came Draska's voice saying quietly, "Seems to be unanimous, doesn't it?"

Eudora's voice had a cold little smile in it. "Why wouldn't it be? You convinced me, Dave, and I'm hard to convince. The same corny something in me that makes me waste my time in drama began thinking of centuries of gallant ladies having babies in the wings and stepping on stage exactly on cue."

"Quiet," said Draska. And, "Out of thirty-two votes, thirty-one are in favor of ringing up the curtain tonight, only one in favor of abandoning the performance!"

One vote again, thought Tuck.

And then began the long procession of strained young faces to the lighted stage where Tuck sat at the small wooden table. Draska had announced Tuck's presence as mildly as possible, never mentioning *murder*, but using instead a string of casual words involving "the usual investigations when the cause of a death is not entirely plain . . . Mr. Tuck wishes to question each of you very briefly . . . Give him your name, because you are of course all strangers to him . . . on stage, as that was simplest. . . ." None of which displeased Tuck.

All but five were disappointments—they had seen Ann Laird the night before, on stage, or in the dressing-room after rehearsal, had or had not exchanged some amenity, and all wanted to know what had happened to Ann, to which Tuck replied, "That's what I hoped you could help me find out."

But from the other five, Tuck was able to piece out what Ann had done on the night she died.

The first to speak to her after the final curtain had been Joe, who revealed that he was head prop man and waited for Tuck to take it on from there.

"When did you last see Mrs. Laird alive?" asked Tuck.

"Right after the final curtain. About eleven o'clock. She got up from the floor where she was lying with Romeo and asked me for the key to the prop room, or was it open. I said the inside door was locked, and I didn't have the key because Miss Fitch—she's the secretary in the Drama Office—gave it away to some screwball professor. I told Ann the outside door was open, but she'd better lock it after her, and I gave her the key and told her to put it on her key ring or something because she loses— that is, she used to lose things right and left. So she said thanks and went down and joined the huddle around Romaine, who was reading off the criticisms of the show she'd jotted down, like she always does. And I got busy bracing the balcony, because it was plenty wobbly."

"Was it customary to leave the prop-room door open?"

"Well, the inside door we always left open because you have to go back and forth quite a bit. But it was locked, so I left the outside door open. I was carrying laths and two-by-fours to brace the balcony with."

"At what time was this?"

"Just before we knocked off for dinner, say about seven."

"By open do you mean open wide, or simply not locked?"

"I guess it was about halfway open—I sort of dragged it to after me with one foot, but it didn't slam."

"So the last time you saw Ann Laird alive was when she was standing with the rest of the cast around Professor Romaine?"

"That's right."

The angular girl who played the nurse said, "She was already out of her costume when I got to the dressing-room, and I was the first one there. Ann was like that—when she did things, she did them fast. Then the other women in the cast came in, and there was a lot of chatter, and I was busy getting my costume and make-up off. I turned to speak to Ann about one of the scenes we had together, and she was gone."

"What time was that?" asked Tuck.

"About eleven-thirty. I remember thinking she must have gone down after that smaller vial Professor Romaine wanted her to use. Well, a few minutes after that, probably about eleven-forty, there was a knock at the door and Dave Draska called, 'We're all going to meet at Carlo's. Anyone who wants a ride had better hurry.' Right after that Meg Fife came in and said that there was room in Oliver's car for one or two more, and wasn't anyone ready to leave? So I told her Ann was, and that if she wasn't in the theater, she was probably down in the prop room. Meg left right away, I thought at the time to get Ann. And that's really all I know."

"Meg Fife and Ann were pretty chummy, then?"

"They had to be. They were the two best actresses around here, and knew it. They were jealous as the devil of each other, and would have died rather than show it."

"I get it." Tuck nodded.

"I voted for Ann for the Juliet part," offered the girl who played the nurse. "Not just because I liked her better, but because she was better as Juliet. Fife could never convince an audience that she was fourteen and in love for the first time. Too darned intellectual. Ann had enthusiasm." She leaned forward. "What has happened to Ann? Besides being killed, I mean."

"What more could happen to Ann?" parried Tuck.

Meg Fife walked with very straight shoulders and a very high head. Her thin mouth was painted a dark red—

really an unpleasant red, thought Tuck—but her fine brown hair with no trace of red or gold in it was hanging artlessly down each side of her pointed face. Her eyes were much too dark in the white face, and had the big, nervous pupils that made Tuck uneasy.

"Good afternoon," she said with composure. Her voice was consciously beautiful.

"Good afternoon. Please sit down."

Meg Fife hesitated and then sat, very gracefully, on the extreme edge of the chair, still holding her square small shoulders very straight and arranging her fine hands nicely. Her feet were well out of sight.

And then, in that lofty, lovely voice, she asked, "Was, she murdered. Mr. Tuck?"

Tuck looked squarely into the big pupils. "Yes."

Meg collapsed just a trifle. Her eyes didn't waver. "Oh. I thought she might have been."

"Why?"

Meg raised a thin, protesting hand. "Oh, I don't mean there was any *reason* she might have been murdered."

"I see," said Tuck. "Well, Miss Fife, here's my problem. I'm trying to piece together what happened last night before she died. I have just learned that you may have gone down to the prop room looking for her at about eleven-forty or so. Did you?"

"It was eleven-forty-five," said Meg clearly. "I looked at my watch. Yes. I went down to the prop room. Is that where she died, Mr. Tuck?"

"Yes."

Meg nodded. "I thought it might have been. I think I got there directly after the murder."

"Dear me," said Tuck. "Why didn't you—?"

"Please let me tell you what happened," commanded Meg Fife. "Paul Ober and Oliver Clarey and I had been—" she pronounced it *bean*,— "having a cigarette on the porch. They decided to go to Oliver's car, parked a block away by the library. Oliver looked at his wrist-watch and said that it was twenty to twelve, and why did women take so long to wipe off some make-up and get out of costume. He suggested I go in to the dressing-room and see if anyone was ready and wanted a ride, and he and Paul would wait in the car by the side entrance of the library. I went straight to the women's dressing-room. No one was ready to leave, and I made some joking remark about it. Then Nora Day—she plays the nurse—said, 'Ann's ready, Meg. She's probably down in the prop room looking for that little silver dingus.' I glanced into the theater first, saw that Ann wasn't there, and so I went down the stairs at the end of the hall. The lights in the basement corridor weren't on, and I remember I thought of going back upstairs again, and then I snapped the switch and went along that long hall to the prop room. To my surprise, the doors were locked. As I turned away, I thought I saw light under the door, so I knocked. There wasn't a sound. I knocked again and called Ann's name. Still no answer. So I started back along the hall. For some reason, I looked back over my shoulder. The end of the basement hall is rather dark, Mr. Tuck, and I could see quite clearly a weak glow of light coming out from under the door. And then, as I looked, the light went out."

"Out," echoed Tuck.

"Yes. I hesitated for a moment, half-inclined to go back and knock again, and then the rather displeasing thought struck me that Ann was in there, all right, had recognized my voice, and for some reason was avoiding me. So I went straight upstairs, and then to the car, and told Oliver and Paul that no one was ready and we might as well get going. We went straight to Carlo's, and got there at about five to twelve. We were the first ones there. At my suggestion, we took one of the big tables on the terrace—it was breathlessly hot, you know. Oliver at once began to worry; he was afraid Ann had not been told where we were going. He talked himself into phoning her house, and came back almost at once with the news that he'd talked to Jim, and she was not home and so undoubtedly intended to join us. On top of that, Dave Draska came in with a horde of people he and Lily had given lifts to, and said yes, Ann knew we were meeting here; he had told her himself, and she said she would come. Another carful was on its way, he said. When they came and Ann wasn't among them Oliver began to get anxious again, and I had to remind him, and sound rather catty doing it, that Ann always had taken full advantage of the female prerogative of changing her mind."

"And you yourself—what did you think was the reason Ann didn't meet you?"

Meg Fife blinked once, the way a kitten blinks. "Just exactly what I said. That she had changed her mind."

Oliver Clarey contributed nothing new except grief. He pushed the curtain violently aside and came across the stage to Tuck with his kinky black head strained forward, his eyebrows like two black feathers almost meeting above the short straight nose. Beads of sweat were on the fine white skin of his forehead; a heavy growth of beard accented the sensual curl of his pale mouth. He planted two strong masculine hands on the little wooden table and strained forward toward Tuck, his light blue eyes glowing with intensity.

"You've got to tell me what's happened," he demanded in a startlingly loud voice. "I can't stand this."

"Someone hit her on the head," said Tuck. "You'd better sit down."

Oliver Clarey fell into the little wooden chair facing Tuck. He sat there asprawl, staring at nothing, and then put one hand up over his eyes. "God!" he groaned. Then he dropped the hand and stared at Tuck. "I knew something was wrong," he said fiercely. One clenched fist went against his flat chest. "I felt it, last night."

"What made you feel it?" asked Tuck.

The fist unclenched. Clarey looked with strange eyes at his hand and then reached into his pocket and brought out a crumpled handkerchief with which he wiped his upper lip. "I don't know."

"Most 'feelings,' " offered Tuck, "are largely a matter of the historical viewpoint. They are 'felt' in retrospect."

"No," said Clarey. "I tell you, it was like being haunted. Ask Paul. Ask Meg Fife."

"She has told me that you were rather worried that Ann wouldn't join the party at Carlo's."

"That was just part of it. It began—it began when we were all waiting in the wings, at the start of dress rehearsal. Ann told me that Professor Romaine had complimented her on her grasp of the part. Ann was in the middle of one of her periods of exaltation—she was always either very up or very down—and she said to me, 'Oh, I am so happy that I'm sure something terrible is going to happen. The gods must be jealous of me.' "

"Yes?"

"Well, at the end of the play—the scene in the tomb, where Romeo says, '*How oft when men are at the point of death Have they been merry! which their keepers call A lightning before death*,'—I suddenly found myself thinking, 'That's Ann!' "

"And," said Tuck, "it seems as though it was."

Suddenly there were tears in Oliver Clarey's eyes. They stared at each other for a moment, and then Clarey got violently up and went away. . . .

Paul Ober sat down quietly. His ease had not deserted him. His smile had. "I've been told," he said, "that someone hit Ann on the head, in the prop room, last night after the show. I haven't the slightest idea who could have done it, or why."

"That's what I call getting to the point," said Tuck.

"How well did you know Mrs. Laird?"

"We've been in the same Advanced Drama class for two semesters. We did a good many scenes together. I liked her—I think she liked me too. My grades took a swoop to a new low last semester, and she gave me some notes she had saved from a Geology course, and she coached me for the final exam. You have to maintain a certain average in order to get parts, and she felt that my laziness might defeat my career. If it hadn't been for her, I wouldn't be playing Romeo, and think what a loss to the world that would be."

"And you didn't notice anything unusual last night?"

"Nothing. Everyone, including Ann, behaved exactly as always. But that in itself is unusual, isn't it?"

"What do you mean?"

"I mean," said Paul Ober, regarding Tuck steadily, "that if one of us killed her, you would think, wouldn't you, that something would show."

It was almost five when the curtains parted for the last time. Eudora stepped through, followed by Draska.

"How did it go?" she asked.

"Everyone was very charming and apparently made great efforts to be helpful. No one said anything nasty about anyone, and they had nothing but good to say of Ann. I might just as well have spent the afternoon playing cribbage with Froody."

"What in the name of heaven is 'froody'?" demanded Draska. "Animal, vegetable, or mineral?"

"Animal," said Eudora gravely. "Mr. Tuck leaves him with corpses. What did you think of the thing on the bulletin board?"

"What thing on what bulletin board?" Tuck asked.

"I haven't had a chance to show him," Draska said.

"Well, come on!" Eudora yelped. Grabbing Tuck's big hand in hers, she led him through the curtain, forced him to follow her in a wild leap over the footlights, and raced him up the sloping aisle of the theater, with Draska loping along in the rear and panting, "Eudora! It'll keep. After all, it's under lock and key!"

They burst through the glass-topped door of the Drama Office across the hall and startled the gentle little lady at a desk at the far end. Eudora bore down on her with extended palm. "The key to the closet, please, Miss Fitch."

Eudora went to a tall oak door, unlocked it and flung it wide. Draska went to her side and helped her lug out a gilt-framed, glass-covered bulletin board. Tuck vaguely remembered having seen it standing in a corner of the porch of Old College that morning when he arrived.

Eudora said earnestly to Tuck, "I think this is very, very important."

Tuck stepped closer. Something was on the bulletin board that had not been there that morning. An advertisement, roughly torn from a newspaper. Below the smudgy photograph of a very black coffin ran the line: "*Of course you want the finest. Bupp-Lambkin, Funeral Directors.*" It had been stuck to the glass with a gob of chewing gum. It hung, a little askew, directly beside a photograph of Ann Laird's smiling face.

Chapter Ten: CHRONIC DELUSIONS

"ALL THESE happy children," said Tuck, "living in a private world as far from reality as the moon from Main Street, and you're trying to tell me one of 'em is mad."

"That's right," said Eudora.

A waitress went past their red and yellow umbrella very fast; Tuck caught the streamer of her apron and drew her gently to their table. "More coffee?" he asked Eudora. She nodded. "Two more coffees," he said to the waitress, who bobbed the starched cap with the red

Carlo's on it, and tied her sash.

Eudora put up one hand, shielding her eyes from the last long rays of the sun. Faint and clear came the sound of the chimes in the tower of the Philosophy Building, striking six. "Paranoia, I should imagine," she said.

"Ah," said Tuck. "Delusions."

"Delusions," agreed Eudora.

"The last paranoic I saw thought he was Winston Churchill," said Tuck. "My friend the psychiatrist faced him with another paranoic. He also thought he was Winston Churchill, and said so. 'What do you think of that?' the psychiatrist asked the first. 'I think,' he said, 'that this fellow is crazy. There can't be *two* Churchills.' "

Eudora nodded amiably. "The last time I heard that story, they both thought they were Napoleon," she said.

"My point is," said Tuck, "that whether they thought they were Churchill, Napoleon, or little white mice, there was no chance of missing the fact that they were crazy."

Eudora pounced. "Ah. That was because the delusion was a striking one. But what if the delusion were not so striking? What if a person who was a good actor simply went a little further and decided he was the greatest actor on earth? What if with this grandiose delusion went an accompanying persecutory delusion? What if, in this distorted mind we're speaking about, Ann Laird gradually became the persecutor? The one person in the world who was standing in our lunatic's sunlight? The one person who was keeping him from the just recognition of his great talent?" She sat back and then leaned impulsively forward again. "You realize, of course, that with pure paranoia, there is no dementia, no hallucination, no emotional disturbance. A paranoic fools himself on the one score—except for that false premise or interpretation, his mind works as a normal mind. He might be an able architect, a competent mathematician or businessman. He would be able to think, and think well, apart from the subject of his delusion.

"That's true," Tuck said slowly.

"Sometimes, of course, the delusion of persecution makes the paranoic—somewhat dangerous."

"Why should Ann Laird have been chosen by the paranoic as his persecutor?"

"I don't know. But there could have been an easy beginning for it. Suppose our paranoic simply told her, one day, that he was the greatest actor on earth. Suppose Ann laughed at him, thinking he was trying to be funny. Suppose that began it. Suppose he—or she—was brooding one day: 'I am a great actor. Better than anyone else around here. Better than those hams getting fat checks from Hollywood.' And then the uneasy other voice inside his mind, 'Well, but if you're so good, why aren't you in Hollywood, or on Broadway?' 'Because people are jealous of me. They don't want me to get ahead.' 'Who doesn't? Who's jealous of you?' 'Ann Laird! She laughed at me. She'd do anything to get ahead herself and push me back! She's jealous of me!' And there you have it, Mr. Tuck."

"So then our paranoic killed her and stuck a coffin to her picture. With chewing gum."

"We don't know what happened in that prop room, Mr Tuck. We don't know what insane accusations were made and how Ann reacted to them. But we do know that some one got mad enough to bash her head in, and not many people are capable of anger like that!"

"And the coffin?"

Eudora closed her eyes for a moment, then opened them and stared intensely into his. "Oh, I can see that so clearly! Can't you see this distorted mind, utterly without grief, opening a paper, seeing that coffin, remembering Ann's smiling face on the porch of Old College? Can't you see him ripping out the ad, stuffing it in his pocket, passing the bulletin board? Then looking quickly about, and with a quick jab, gluing the coffin to the picture of the person he hated enough to kill? I can, Mr. Tuck."

Tuck was thinking of the voice on the telephone: *Your wife is dead, and I know who killed her. . . .*

"A gesture of triumph," Eudora was saying. "A gesture possible only to a distorted brain."

Tuck sat in the next-to-the-end seat in the last row of Touchstone Theater. A portly gentleman in dinner clothes, whom he took to be the head of the Drama Department, announced that the part of Juliet would be taken, not by Ann Laird, as the programs said, but by Meg Fife. The house lights dimmed and went out, and slowly the red curtains drew apart, and it was Verona, a public place.

Romeo had just entered when someone slipped into the empty aisle seat next to Tuck's. It was Professor Romaine. She abstractedly loosened the dark fluffy fur from around her shoulders, her eyes glued to the stage.

And the play went on. By intermission it seemed to Tuck that the performances he was seeing on the little stage were far from amateurish. He guessed where most of the credit was due, and complimented Professor Romaine on her excellent direction.

Her lips pursed in the reverse of any smile he had ever seen, and she said, "I have seen Romeo played better only once. I had nothing to do with that, either."

'How about Juliet?" he asked.

She turned on him the full force of her dark eyes. Then she looked intently at the bald head of a man three rows down. "Of course," she said, "I have always wanted to see the play done with no Juliet at all. Just Romeo, speaking both their lines. The young man and his dream."

While Tuck assimilated this, the lights went out.

The last act was the best. Paul Ober's melancholy face came into its own; as he drank the poison in a blue pool of light, he somehow turned his head so that, for just an instant, those clear eyes of his caught light and held it, and then closed.

"Oh, bravo!" Professor Romaine whispered.

When the curtain closed there was genuine applause in the little theater. Before the lights went on, Professor Romaine slipped out as silently as she had entered. Tuck followed her. She was going rapidly down the dim corridor toward the porch when Tuck called her name. She paused and turned, the way a mannequin turns, on the balls of her feet. She was completely in black, and he saw that she had once been very beautiful. In that moment, she was beautiful again. But she darted her eyes restlessly toward the door and looked back at him reluctantly.

"How did they do it?" he asked. "Why wasn't this like every other amateur play I've ever seen?"

After a glance at the door, she suddenly was moving toward him, her slim black gown almost motionless as she walked. She reached him and passed him, and turned again, backed by the utilitarian burlap of the screens which walled off the dressing-rooms. Then she raised one long ivory finger and beckoned mysteriously.

Surprised, he slowly went to her. She went to one of the screens, opened one flap as though she was opening a door, and passed through. He followed in complete bafflement. Behind the screens, she carefully closed the space by which they had entered, just as the first of the audience streamed out of the theater into the hall. Then she opened her large black purse, fumbled in it for a moment, and drew out a platinum cigarette case. She took out a cigaret and lighted it. She drew in smoke and expelled it.

"Teaching has its disadvantages," she said.

Then came the flat sound of a door closing, and Paul Ober came toward them from the wings, his well-shaped legs moving swiftly in their black tights, his eyes light and brilliant against the dark make-up on his face.

He gave them his quick salute and started up the stairs to the men's dressing-rooms.

"Paul!" called Professor Romaine, in her deep voice. He turned swiftly, one hand on the wide balustrade.

"Paul, you were *good*," said Professor Romaine.

"Thanks. I thought Meg did awfully well."

"Meg," said Professor Romaine, "played Meg as well as I've ever seen it played."

Paul smiled. "A man in the loudest sport coat I've ever seen was on stage as soon as the curtain fell saying things to her about a screen test."

"Splendid!" said Professor Romaine warmly. "But you, Paul, were *good*."

Tuck left, knowing that Professor Romaine was determined to behave as though Death had not made an unexpected entrance into her world. He decided that this reaction, so unusual for a woman, probably sprang from a helpless grief that had to be ignored by a mind completely conscious of its ultra-sensitivity.

The squad room was empty, except for Froody, a dumpy little figure sitting sadly at a desk under the hard lights. "You told me I should wait," he said with dignity. "A man telephoned you, but he wouldn't leave a message with me. Oh, no. Not with me."

"Froody," said Tuck, "why don't I get any nice easy cases, with the murderer losing his head and shouting, 'Yes, I killed her! And I'm glad, glad, glad!'"

"Why do I always hold the bag?" asked Froody. "Some things just happen to some people."

"What did the doctor have to say?"

Froody opened a black notebook exactly like Tuck's, licked his thumb and pushed back some pages. "She died," he read, "from a heavy blow just above the occipital bone, causing a concave fracture of both parietal bones of the cranium, and considerable damage to the brain tissue. She has been dead not less than six hours and not more than fourteen."

"Could the blow have been caused by striking her head against that iron dumbbell?"

"Only if she struck it plenty hard, he said. She couldn't have just slipped and fallen onto it. He couldn't say about the body having been moved. If so, it happened before rigor began to set in."

Froody turned the page. "*Res gestae* evidence," he announced with some pride. "One white dress. One slip. One pair of shorts. One pair of green shoes. Stockings. Garters. One green purse. In the purse: one comb, three teeth missing; one compact; one lipstick; four keys on a silver chain; one key—the one to the outer door of the room where body was found; three brown bobby pins; one box of mascara; one fountain pen; one piece of ruled paper, folded. On this was written: 'Wear lower heels. Get smaller vial. Shorter pause before stabbing. Butter. Eggs. Bacon.' "

"No small, flat automatic, you'll notice," said Tuck. "No small, leather-covered diary. No letter from someone signing himself, 'Ever thine, Alonzo.' "

"Nope. Just what I told you. The dress had some dust on it from the floor. And a couple of reporters came along —I gave 'em the usual magoo."

"Have you seen the photos yet?"

"No."

"I'll take a look at em tomorrow. Fingerprints?"

"Lots of em."

"How about that light switch by the door? They got a print from that?"

"Yeah. One half of one thumb, and smudged."

"Man or woman, would you say?"

Froody shrugged. "What did you find out?"

Tuck told him what he had found out.

"A nut, this York thinks, huh?" brooded Froody.

"Yes. And I have to admit that business with the coffin doesn't look too sane to me." Tuck fished into his inner breast pocket and drew out an envelope. He handed the coffin advertisement to Froody. "You might find out what paper that was torn from, for whatever good that'll do us. Of course, it doesn't necessarily follow that the person who killed her, and the man who phoned Jim Laird, and the person who stuck the coffin to the bulletin board are all the same person."

"No," agreed Froody. "But then you're worse off. Because then you've got someone that bats a nice young lady on the head, *and* someone who pins a coffin to her picture, *and* someone who phones her husband and gloats about the fact that she's dead. I, personally, would rather have them all the same guy."

"That wouldn't be so bad if it weren't for the campus angle. Because you've got not only a mental case, but a mental case who goes around among his friends from class to class, and yet never tips off the fact that he's crazy."

"Listen," said Froody. "I've seen nuts that were definitely charming people."

"But still, I can't help thinking that *someone* would have noticed certain deviations from normal; that *someone* would have stumbled on this lunatic's delusion. Because once he got started on that, the fact that he was wacky on one subject would have been very plain."

"Maybe someone did," said Froody. "Maybe Ann Laird did."

The telephone on the desk rang. Tuck picked up the receiver. "Tuck speaking."

An operator's voice said, "Here is your party. Kindly signal when through."

"This is Laird, Mr. Tuck," said a voice that was carefully controlled, a voice that nevertheless showed strain.

"I'm calling from my folks house in Hawthorne. This seems important. I've been thinking about that phone call I got when you were at the apartment this afternoon. There was something funny about that voice, Mr. Tuck.

The more I think about it, the more I think that it could have been a woman trying to sound like a man."

Chapter Eleven: MURDERERS IN HASTE

THAT AFTERNOON Millicent left to spend the week-end with an aunt. Eudora studied until six, had dinner, and went to a motion-picture theater near campus.

Sunday she found herself thinking of her enthusiastic conviction of Friday night that Ann Laird's murderer was not sane. And today that explanation for some reason was not as satisfactory as it had been then. *Of course, she thought, when I was spouting all those words to Tuck, I was under the immediate influence of that coffin advertisement. Now, while I still can't get away from the fact that the person who tore that out of a paper and gummed it up beside Ann's picture certainly had a malignant sense of humor, and certainly disliked Ann, I'm not so sure that he need be crazy, and I'm not so sure he killed her. Then, I was not thinking so much as reacting intuitively. Now I'm beginning to want a little more concrete proof. Or I at least want someone whose opinion I can respect to agree with my theory. I'm not at all sure Tuck did.*

Professor Brewer! she thought. *He knows as much as I do about the murder. I don't like him, but he's a trained psychologist, certainly the logical person for me to present my paranoic theory to for confirmation.*

She knew that he lived in a bachelor apartment, some- where near campus, because of certain crass undergrad- uate stories which wild-fired from psychology student to psychology student, all concerned with Professor Brewer, his bachelor apartment, and impressionable female Sopho- mores. Eudora had paid little attention—she had learned that undergraduate wit is callow and thoughtless.

She found Brewer's name in the telephone book; after three rings his hard, quick voice said, "Yes?"

"This is Eudora York, Professor Brewer."

"Oh, yes. What is it, please?"

"I'd like to talk to you about the murder." A silence at the other end of the wire—so she went on: "Something rather odd has happened—I think it's right up your alley."

"My alley," said Professor Brewer, "is Abnormal Psychology. As far as murder is concerned, Miss York, I am more or less of an amateur, unless the murder is such that the advice of an alienist is necessary."

"Yes. That's why I'm phoning you."

"Oh?" The brisk voice was lukewarm with interest. "Look, Miss York. I realize that we can't discuss this over the phone, but please tell me this much: Am I right in guessing that this odd incident you spoke about suggests that the murderer is insane?"

"Yes."

A pause. "I am free until five o'clock. If you wish it, I'm willing to see you at once. May I suggest my apartment?"

"Fine," said Eudora. "I'll see you in ten minutes." *Your apartment*, she thought, as she hung up. *Hmmm.*

But Professor Brewer's apartment was innocuous in the extreme. There were no etchings on the wall (campus rumor), nor did Professor Brewer greet her in a black velvet lounging robe (another report), nor did he keep two candles burning before a portrait of Sigmund Freud. A bag of golf clubs leaned in one corner, with their reassuring suggestion of healthy outdoor sport.

Brewer was wearing the same dark suit he wore in class, and the large flat-topped desk gave an office-like atmosphere to the room. With what she considered exceedingly good taste, he underscored the businesslike nature of their meeting by seating himself in the swivel chair of the desk after having politely seated her in a leather club chair facing it. He offered her a cigarette, which she refused, lighted one himself, and began to smoke in jerky puffs. A metal desk lamp shed its pool of light on the green blotter and the pens and pencils, and sharpened the bright green of Eudora's suit.

She immediately told him about the mortuary advertisement, and her conclusions therefrom.

Professor Brewer delicately tipped the long ash of his cigarette into a big brass tray on the desk. She noticed his hands for the first time, and they disturbed her, because they did not match the pointed face. They were small fat hands, and they should have been thin.

"Well," said Brewer, in his classroom voice, "let's see what arguments support your theory. What time was it when you found this ad stuck to the bulletin board?"

"About twelve-thirty on Friday. And it wasn't there when I left you at the start of Chapel Hour, because I stood looking at the bulletin board for several minutes and certainly would have seen it."

"And by twelve-thirty how many people, besides you, and Barney, and Tuck and the other detective, and I, knew of the murder?"

"As far as I know, only Draska. Oh, and you had told President Trinklehaus."

Brewer gave his thin smile. "I think we can safely say he had no hand in it. I know I didn't do it. You didn't. Barney says he didn't. Draska, you say, was staggered when he discovered it. So it begins to look as though the only person who could have gummed that coffin ad to Ann's picture is the murderer."

"Yes. Tuck and I went over that after I showed it to him. What I want to know is this: Was I too hasty in assuming that a murderer who attaches a picture of a coffin to the picture of the person he killed is insane?"

"I will say he certainly has an odd sense of humor. I'd like a little more evidence before going further."

Eudora edged forward on her chair. "Well, I'll tell you why I was so quick to jump at the idea of insanity. Ann is my roommate's closest friend. Millicent adores her. I know her only through Millie, and so I can't speak from my own knowledge. But from all I've heard, she was a pretty swell gal. In other words, there doesn't seem to be any suggestion of a normal motive for killing her. But here's the big difficulty. The murderer must have known she was going to the prop room, and the only way he could know was by being at rehearsal. That's what bothers me. It's hard to imagine one of the people I see every day is insane."

"What made you leap to the conclusion of paranoia?"

"Just that. I was trying to think of a mental disorder which would not be too apparent, and with which there would be no mental deterioration."

"Paranoia is not the only possibility. I'll come back to that. Do you know what interests me more than anything else about this affair? The basic factors of place, time and method. From those three factors, you get a fairly clear notion of this crime. The place was secluded, which at first glance suggests a rendezvous. That's eliminated by the girl's own character, as well as by the fact that she let everyone know she was going there after rehearsal. However, as you've suggested, it might have been a one-sided rendezvous; someone might have taken advantage of that opportunity to talk to Ann Laird alone."

"Or to kill her."   •

"Or to kill her. So he either had something to say to her of a private nature, or something to do to her of a private nature—that being murder. The time seems to dovetail, because the lateness of the hour was further guarantee of no interruption. Now the method—a blow on the back of the head. Here we come to something interesting. You remember, of course, Mr. Tucker's dramatic bit of business with the light. With no disrespect to him, my suggestion is that the light was not necessarily turned off *after* she was struck. It could have been turned off *before* she was hit, by the murderer, as he entered through that outer door!"

"But why?"

"The weapon used! A heavy, blunt object. Even a layman knows that death by a blow on the head is not always immediate. By turning out the light, he prevented Ann from recognizing him, and later identifying him in case she should linger before dying, or not die at all!"

"I see," said Eudora slowly. This idea struck an uneasy note far back in her brain, like the metallic shiver of a far gong being struck. The suggestion of that small forethought on the part of the murderer made Ann Laird's dying horrible.

Brewer mashed out his cigarette. "It's only an idea—no way of knowing whether it's what really happened."

"No. But if it did, a theory that's been building up inside my head while we've been talking is eliminated."

Brewer smiled a little patronizingly. "You've listened to my theory, so I'll listen to yours."

"Well, there's one outstanding fact about Ann that is peculiar to her alone. And I can't help thinking it may have played a part in her murder. She was married."

Two deep vertical creases appeared between Brewer's dark eyebrows. "You're not suggesting the husband is—?"

"She was in love with her husband, Professor."

His frown deepened.

"There may have been someone in love with her who, in the grip of a powerful infatuation, did or said something that caused an equally powerful denial on Ann's part. Someone who, in the grip of a gigantic frustration, released all his thwarted energy by killing her on the spot."

To her surprise, he smiled. "I think, Miss York, you overestimate the effect of frustration on the average male."

"I don't believe I do," she said coolly. "If you happen to recall, Freud, in his *Introduction to Psychoanalysis*, makes the point that although most people's censored desires escape through dreams, one cannot underestimate the psychopathic power of frustration."

Brewer smiled again. "You're right. However—"

Eudora interrupted. "You can see why I say that your idea—that the light could have been turned off first—breaks my theory down. For my theory to work, the murder would have been a matter of spontaneous combustion."

"I agree. Of course, the coffin ad is not explained."

"Oh, yes. Because then the coffin ad was used by a sane person to suggest that the person who killed Ann was not sane."

Brewer lit another cigarette, looking down into the match's flame. Then he said, "Your theory is of course a theory. There's no proof."

"Well, there *are* the cigarette butts, of course."

"Cigarette butts? Don't tell us that our murderer has been leaving a trail of cigarette butts."

"On Friday morning Lieutenant Tuck found five beside that bench outside the prop room. I saw them. They hadn't been there long. He said they'd been dewed on, which suggests that they were probably smoked sometime the night before. That doesn't mean they were smoked by the murderer, but if they were, it means someone waited outside the prop room for Ann, and it might even mean that the person who waited was disturbed about something. Because unless you smoke them very fast, one after the other, it takes a long time to smoke five cigarettes. The fact that he left them there argues in favor of a non-premeditated murder."

Brewer, nodding a little impatiently, said, "Your notion that the murderer was mentally unsound interests me more. As a matter of fact, these arguments you have just given in favor of your frustration idea actually support the other theory. Because I still say you overestimate the effects of frustration on the average man."

"I wasn't thinking of an average man."

"Exactly. So we come right back to our mentally unsound murderer, don't you see?"

Eudora nodded, a little dazed at his deft manipulation of her arguments.

Brewer continued, "Perhaps the reason I like the first theory better is that in thinking about this crime I had come somewhat to the same conclusion."

Eudora smothered a desire to say, *Why didn't you say so?* and contented herself with looking modestly triumphant.

Brewer saw the look and raised a plump, protesting hand. "Not paranoia. But I did do some thinking about constitutional pathological inferiority."

Eudora's mind scrambled back over her lecture notes of the past semester in search of the meaning of the words. Before she found it, Brewer said, "Moral insanity or moral imbecility." He grinned. "Remember now?" Before she could reply, a serious look came over his face and he said, "The antisocial acts of a pathological inferior run the gamut from queerness to criminality. The most emphasized features are constant egocentricity, impulsiveness, inconsistency of conduct, and a peculiar failure to evaluate the consequences of actions. And here's something more to the point. C.P.I.'s can appear in any walk of life. They may have a low or a very high intelligence. They may be socially quite charming."

Once more that faint gong sounded in Eudora's mind. "I didn't know that pathological inferiority extended to murder."

"Oh, yes. Murders in haste, usually. Clumsy, bungling murders. And very often with amazingly slender provocation." He looked at his watch.

Eudora stood up. "Thank you for your time. It's rather nice to know I wasn't entirely wrong....."

She left Professor Brewer's apartment strangely depressed, for no reason that she could determine.

Chapter Twelve: SUPPER BY CANDLELIGHT

THREE MINUTES later, as Eudora slid open the door of the little automatic elevator to step out into the dark first-floor hall, she found herself face to face with Meg Fife. A glow was under Meg's pallid skin, as though she might have walked for a long time, but her eyes were somber. She was carrying a large paper bag from which celery flourished. Embarrassing, smiling hesitation, and then Meg stepped aside so Eudora could leave the elevator. She then contrived to hold the door open so Meg could enter. Under the hard top light of the elevator, Meg's face looked tired.

To Eudora's considerable surprise, Meg said, "Look. If you're not doing anything, why not have supper with me?"

Eudora sensed an urgency in Meg's cool voice which interested her. "I'd love to." And as they were riding upward, "I didn't know you lived here. I thought you were in that boardinghouse on Thirty-sixth."

"There is nothing," Meg stated, "more horrible than the voices of many women. I can't afford this really, but I fool myself by promising to get a roommate, which I won't do until the wolf has kittens on the doorstep."

They got out on the floor Eudora had just left. Meg walked down the hall in the opposite direction from Brewer's apartment, balanced the bundle on one hip while she fished a key from the pocket of her tan coat, and unlocked the door. "I think it's going to rain," she said as she crossed the darkness of the room and switched on a lamp.

The room was almost bare of homelike touches. Like a man's room, it seemed to be for eating, dressing and sleeping. With the exception of books heaped about every horizontal surface, the only mark of Meg she could see was a large, gold-framed portrait of Meg over the sofa. Eudora, partly for something to do and partly out of interest in the unusual technique, which suggested that the artist had half-closed his eyes and placed daubs of raw color here and there, stood looking up at the picture while Meg disposed of her bundle in the kitchen. Since she could not say the picture was good, she said, "Who did the portrait of you?"

"Oh," said Meg from the kitchen. "You guessed it was me. Most people don't, or not so soon. It was done by a chap I used to know in Greenwich Village. He was experimenting with a new technique. Do you like canned asparagus in your salad?"

"I'm very omnivorous," said Eudora, and walked idly to a long table, opening one of the books. It was Millay's translation of Baudelaire's *Fleurs du Mal,* and on the flyleaf bore the sentiment in a strong masculine hand: *For Mélisande Borgia from the ever-admiring Charles.* Meg's voice startled her by its closeness. She turned her head and saw her standing just behind her, tying a businesslike apron behind her back.

"Charles," she said, "now has three lovely children." There was something weary in her smile as she added, "He used to enjoy thinking that I looked like a cross between Mélisande and Lucrezia Borgia. My face is not my fortune, Eudora. Every man I've known has seen something different in it, and has married a plump blonde who at once started having babies. Will a large salad and a steak and hot rolls be enough? If you say the word, I'll open a can of something else."

"That'll be more than sufficient," and, as Meg turned back toward the kitchen, she added, "Let me help."

"Nothing to do. The salad's made. I'll slap the steaks under the broiler and hurl the rolls into the oven, and we'll be eating in five minutes. Oh, and I have some rather nice sherry, for festivity."

It did not seem much more than five minutes before they were sitting opposite each other at a tiny table in the boxlike dinette. Meg had lighted two dribbled candles in shiny brass candlesticks, and as Eudora saw Meg sitting there, she knew that Meg had sat at many small tables by candlelight, with many different people, and had always been alone even as she looked across into their eyes. Meg raised her glass of wine to admire its color, and the gesture was a man's gesture; Eudora was quite sure that Meg's reasons would be a man's reasons—would involve the goal in view and not the passing moment.

The wine was good. Eudora had been wondering why Meg was going to this trouble, which did not seem like Meg, but the taste of the wine made such ideas somehow shameful, and she said sincerely, "I should have congratulated you sooner on the screen test. Paul told me about it. I think it's splendid."

Meg was sipping wine. She lowered the glass swiftly to the table and sat looking at her hand holding the slim stem. "Do you?" Her voice was flat. She looked out the window at the fog. Then she looked at Eudora. "I'm afraid," she said.

The fear in her voice meant more than the words, and Eudora felt a sympathetic twinge. A curious excitement flooded her. In her mind clear and sharp and three-dimensional, she saw Ann Laird's dead body with the dark red blotch beneath the broken skull. She made her voice steady and clinical. "What are you afraid of. Meg?"

Meg looked down into her wine. raised the glass and drank some. "I don't know. I've tried to tell myself that I'm seeing the slow crumbling of a philosophy of life which I and all my generation believed to be the only one. There's khaki everywhere now, you hear soldiers marching past your window early in the morning and late at night you hear their voices singing in the streets. Everywhere the individual and his aims and plans are growing less and less important. I try to tell myself that's what frightens me. Sometimes I listen to a news report on the radio late at night, and realize that the world is changed from the world I thought would always be there, and I feel like a ghost that's come back after a long lapse of time." She gave a rough sketch of a laugh. "I've always been sorry for ghosts, haven't you? Even as a child they couldn't frighten me. I always have felt that they were the ones who must be frightened." Meg looked up at Eudora and down into her glass again.

"And is that all?" asked Eudora.

Meg shook her head. "No. It's Ann—her death frightens me."

"Why?"

Meg's eyes looked into hers. "I don't know."

The baselessness of the fear was more impressive to Eudora than a fear with a reason would have been. Eudora found herself thinking, *She has to step into the spotlight. She's deluding herself deliberately.* Meg seemed to sense that the scene was at an end, for she said, "Women are very foolish and I sometimes think actresses are the worst. We feed on our own emotion to an extent that's almost obscene, don't we?"

But her face there in the candlelight had in it still some of the strain Eudora had noticed in the elevator. It was an old strain, as though it belonged there; as though the passive powdered face with the dark lips that went in and out of classes was a mask. She recalled that Meg was taking her Ph.D. in Drama. That meant a good many years of college. That meant a good many years of life for Meg. More, certainly, than the little pointed face and the childishly casual hair would suggest.

"Meg," she asked quietly, "how old are you?"   ♦

"Twenty-six," said Meg, looking levelly at Eudora. Eudora was quite sure she was lying. Then Meg grinned. She had a sudden, triangular smile that could be called nothing else. "But if anything comes of this screen test, I'll go back to twenty-one." She rose briskly and picked up the two empty plates.

Eudora sat staring at a candle flame. *Greenwich Village. When lafe was lafe and looove was looove. That was a long time ago.*

They went into the living-room and by the light of one lamp listened to a program of classical music. Meg was very quiet. Eudora could not clear her head of the idea that she was glad for company. When she at last rose to go, Meg's protests were certainly sincere, but Eudora was not flattered, for she had the notion that any human being would have served Meg's purpose. They heard the fine spat of rain on the windowpane.

"I'll lend you my raincoat," said Meg matter-of-factly.

"Don't bother, please. It's only a few blocks over to the dorm, and it's raining very lightly."

But Meg emerged from the closet with a yellow slicker. Eudora thought, as she slipped into it, *That little child angle again—like the hair.* "I really don't need this," she objected, but her deep hatred for borrowing was not proof against Meg's generous consideration. Feeling like a large yellow omnibus, she walked out of the apartment building into a cool night of glistening pavements.

When she reached the muggy little foyer of the dormitory, the student at the desk looked up and said, "Oh, wait. There was a phone call for you. I wrote it down." She handed Eudora a half-sheet of lined paper on which she had written in her curly schoolgirl handwriting: *Lieutenant Tuck phoned and wishes you to meet him at nine o'clock at the outer door of the prop room. He says will you please get ahold of a key.*

The clock above the desk said ten minutes to nine.

Eudora walked down University Avenue with a jumble of thoughts in her head. *Sunday night on campus always has a lonely feel. The library is dark, and so are the buildings, and the street lamps seem to emphasize the solitude. I wonder what he wants. I hope Miss Fitch is home. And I hope she brought the keys home with her.*

But Miss Fitch was not home. Her little bungalow a half-block from Old College was dark.

With her cold hands inside the clammy pockets of Meg's yellow slicker, Eudora hurried along the side street toward University Avenue and its lights. From the busy city that surrounded the quiet campus she could hear the faint swish of car tires on wet streets, but the rain seemed to close the campus in more securely. She felt a sudden affection for this small world where she had spent three years. *This won't change,* she told herself, and realized that Meg's verbal essay about the war had gone rather deep into her mind.

Old College in the rain—the night and the building went together. The gray old façade with its grandeur from the century just past, with its parasitic vines, had never seemed impressive before. But tonight she stood staring at it, there at the place where the side street joined University, waiting for a roll of thunder. But nothing happened except the light rain, falling steadily.

As she stepped onto the squishy grass and walked toward the side of the building under the tall dripping elms, she wished she had worn her rubbers. That practical thought was in her mind when something crashed against her skull with a queer round sound that had pain in it. The last things she was conscious of were a taste in her mouth like blood and the soggy ground hitting her cheek.

Chapter Thirteen: A LAMP AND A COLD

TUCK STOOD on the porch of the Laird home, saying good-by. The Lairds were not a family to 'ake good-bys lightly, even in the midst of tragedy. Mr. Laird, a big, handsome man who in sadness looked a little like a St.

Bernard, stood with his arm across his son's shoulders. Mrs. Laird, a small, pretty woman with iron-gray hair, was still talking, and still had nothing to say. Jim Laird stood between them, wearing that look of oldness which Tuck had seen appear in the little empty apartment on Friday. With their lighted living-room at their backs, they were very solidly a family unit.

As Tuck drove through the twisted pass to Los Angeles, he thought over the little he had learned. Ann Laird had no close relatives. A cousin in New York was an actor, a half-sister in San Francisco was something of a socialite—whom Ann had not seen for many years. Her father's small estate had seen her through college. If there was any mysterious passage in Ann's life prior to her marriage to Jim, it was unknown to any of them. "And I don't think there was," Mrs. Laird had offered, with bright sadness. "Ann was in many ways a very fine person." *It all keeps coming back to the campus,* he thought. *Like Alice, whatever path I take leads me smack into the house again, and what I want is the lovely garden with no paranoic as bright as a button and as mad as a hatter.*

Eudora opened her eyes and rain fell into them. She was lying on her back under an elm tree, but the sparse branches were no protection. Her mouth still tasted of blood. She brushed a finger against her tongue, and it came away red. She lay there and let the rain wash her finger clean. *I must have bitten my tongue,* she thought idly, as though the matter were of minor importance. The back of her head hurt. The back of the inside of her head. *Well,* she thought, still in that languorous and dreamy fashion, *I guess I'd better get up.*

She started to raise her head, and then a sharp thought, as blinding as a fork of lightning, struck through her mind: *People with concussions sometimes get up and walk around a while and say, "I feel fine," and then drop dead.*

She lowered her head to the soaking grass with infinite caution. *I'll stay here,* she thought grimly, *until someone comes.*

She closed her eyes against the rain, and moving her arms as though they were made of glass, tried to close the front opening of the slicker. *Although my stomach has been less wet in the bathtub,* she thought wryly.

She lay there forever, and could literally feel her ears twitch their atrophied muscles at every sound. Thoughts swam in and out of her brain in lazy circles like goldfish in a bowl.

Why me? I'm such a nice person. "This is a terrible thing," said President Trinklehaus. "Miss York was such a nice person." I wonder what he hit me with. And why? And where's Lieutenant Tuck?

I wish someone would come.... Wow! What if someone comes, but what if it's someone coming back?

She lay quietly on the grass and began measuring her chances. *If he left thinking I'm a goner, there's no reason to suppose he'll return. If he's watching, though, and saw me move...* The thought made her sick. Not frightened, just quite simply sick at her stomach. She looked at the other side of the problem: *I don't know how hard he hit me. I don't know how long I've been out cold—very cold. The street lamps are still on, so it's before twelve, and that's all I know. It might be that I could get up and walk home and never be the worse for it. On the other hand, I might fall over suddenly, tomorrow or the next day, or die in my sleep. There's something very paltry about dying in your sleep.*

Then those atrophied muscles of her ears tried to twitch again. Far down the street came the sound of a man's voice, singing. As it came closer, she could distinguish the words. She was afraid to raise her battered head, but she waited until whoever was passing seemed to reach a spot directly before the tree below which she was lying.

"Help!" she called, as loudly as she dared. She felt the blood rush up to her head.

The singing abruptly ceased.

"In here!" she called. "Under the trees."

Came the sound of feet squashing across the lawn. She peered down over her cheeks and saw a man in a trench coat and a limp felt hat. He got closer and closer, and larger and larger, indistinguishable against the light from the street lamps beyond him. Then he was standing over her, looking down with incredulous light eyes.

It was Oliver Clarey. "Holy cow," he said in his big voice. "What happened to you?"

"I think someone tried to kill me," she said calmly. She couldn't help being a little proud of that calmness.

It was worse than ever, waiting for him to phone the Receiving Hospital, but he was back sooner than she dared hope, and squatted companionably down beside her. "I got a half-pint of whisky," he said. "You'd better take a swig. It might help ward off pneumonia."

She eyed the bottle cautiously. If she choked—on the other hand, she felt as though she must be blue clear through. "I wonder if it'll prevent mildew, too?"

He tilted the bottle carefully to her lips. "No, wait!" she said. "I've just remembered. You should never give an accident victim stimulants."

"Then I'll take some," said Clarey, and did. He screwed the top onto the small flask and tucked it into a hip pocket. He said, "I don't like this."

"Neither do I." She could dimly make out his face under the dripping brim of a very old hat.

The pale lips were pressed together, and the eyes were on her face. "When were you hit?"

"Nine o'clock. What time is it now?"

He shot suddenly to his feet, pointing toward the sidewalk. "Good Lord! I walked right past here at nine o'clock. I remember the chimes ringing! I walked right past, singing my head off."

"You may be the reason," said Eudora dryly, "why someone won't stumble over my scarcely recognizable body on his way to an eight o'clock."

Oliver jammed his hands suddenly into the pockets of his trench coat. "Why?" he demanded in a loud, hard voice. "First Ann, now you. Why?"

"You took the words right out of my head."

Oliver stiffened his arms, as though he had shivered. "A lovely person like Ann—ended. Why?"

"Stop!" commanded Eudora. She could sense Oliver's emotions welling up, and she preferred to have him suffer in privacy. Then she heard the wail of the approaching ambulance, and Oliver ran to wave it to a stop.

The doctor at the Receiving Hospital said, after examining her head minutely, "You'll have a lump as big as an egg tomorrow—and a bad cold."

Oliver, who had insisted on riding down with her in the ambulance and was waiting in the hallway outside the half-open door of the ward, called out, "Can she go home?"

"Sure," said the doctor. "No reason why not. I'd stay in bed tomorrow, though, if I were you."

"Still," said Eudora, as she rose from the cot, "there might have been something worse than a bump. Some women have thin skulls which, when struck smartly with a blunt weapon, break like eggshells."

"Come on," called Oliver, pain in his voice. "I'll take you home." Eudora was sorry for her flippancy. "Thank you, Oliver," she said, quite gently.

They stopped at the first drugstore, and she phoned the Homicide Bureau, but Tuck was not there. So she and Oliver rode through the gleaming night on a grinding streetcar. Oliver walked with her to the dormitory.

"Thank you, Oliver," she said again.

He made an expansive gesture. "Any time." He managed to grin, and went down the steps of the porch.

She took a hot bath and went to bed. In spite of her thoughts, which were stepping on each other's heels, she had little trouble in falling asleep. She heard Millicent come in. She bumped her overnight case against the door and then whispered, "Asleep?"

"Mmmm-mmmm," replied Eudora, and was.

Before she opened her eyes she heard the flat and dreary sound of rain falling. But drearier than the rain was a sense of foreboding which haunted her up from the abyss of sleep. Millicent was not in the room. She turned her head with an effort and looked at the clock on the table beside her bed: 7:30. Millicent was at breakfast. She reached up a hand and felt the lump.

What was that dream she'd had? She had been wearing a dress, something like a nightgown and something like a bridal gown, and she had walked eternally through a wood made up of tall thin trees that surrounded Old College: she had been both escaping something and looking for something. Fleeing and pursuing, in a white dress. That had been her dream. In a white dress.

Quite suddenly, she knew what she had hunted and what she had fled. "Ames!" she whispered.

She saw his face leaning toward her, with the discreet sounds of dining about them, the tall dark neck of the wine bottle between them. She heard him say, almost placidly, "Someday I'll kill you."

"Wait, now! Wait!" she told herself. But her thoughts would not be commanded. Rebelliously, they struggled into a form as grotesque as a thing in nightmare.

Ames was attracted by her. Of that there could be no doubt. Whether the attraction he felt deserved the word "love" did not matter. For a month before his trip to Florida she had avoided him, giving him quite candidly her reason: He was not her sort of person because she could find nothing in him to admire. Upon his return, he

had forced her to dine with him, undoubtedly believing
that an absence of two months must have made her heart
grow fonder. At dinner, for the first time, she had bluntly
told him how he looked to her, and left him. Left him
to smash a bottle of wine in a gutter.

He knew she was on props for the play. He had been
graduated from this University a year ago, and undoubtedly knew where the prop room was. Someone had
waited there quite a long time, the night Ann Laird was
killed. Long enough to smoke five cigarettes. She could
see Ames, sitting on that bench beneath that tree, smoking,
waiting patiently—with something heavy, perhaps. A
wrench from his father's car?

But he wouldn't know I would come to the prop room.
No, he took a chance on that. If not—well, there would
be other times. ·

So there Ames sat. And then a figure in a white dress
("I told you once that white's not your color. . . . ") came
around from the front of the building, and opened the
door of the prop room, and went in. The light went on,
and there with her back to Ames stood a smallish girl in
a white dress, with a long brown bob. And then Ames
walked slowly across the grass. ("The light could have
been turned off *before* she was hit, by the murderer, as he
walked in through that outer door. . . . ") And with his
eyes riveted to the girl's back, Ames turned out the light.
. . . ("The most emphasized features are constant egocentricity, impulsiveness, inconsistency of conduct, and a
peculiar failure to evaluate the consequences of actions
. . . socially quite charming . . . quite charming . . . murders in haste . . . amazingly slight provocation. . . . ")

"No," Eudora said aloud. *Maybe,* said a voice inside
her head. And then the morning papers. And another try.
And a man passing, singing. And then?

Granted that her brutal frankness at dinner had turned
his feeling toward her to the acid, corrosive hate of the

egocentric, would such hate be sustained? Would it be sustained beyond the breaking of the wine bottle? Beyond the breaking of Ann Laird's head? That would depend on the pride of the hater. Was Ames proud? She heard his arrogant voice, saw the vanity of his dress—the silken shirt, the beautiful coat.

She closed her eyes. The door opened.

"Eudora!" said Millicent's shrill voice. "Whatever is the matter with you? I tried to wake you but you just muttered at me. You're going to be late to class if you don't get up!"

Eudora opened her eyes and quietly hated the crack in the plaster ceiling for a moment. She slowly sat up and held her head in both hands. "Ohhhh!" she moaned.

"Eudora! What's wrong!"

Eudora spoke loudly. "Dothing! Dothing's wrong!"

"Why, you've got a cold!"

"Yes. I've got a code."

"Your eyes! They're all puffed together!"

Eudora made a swift decision to belittle her condition and get rid of Millicent as soon as possible. "My eyes may dot be large, but they're rheumy," she confided.

"And why all this early-morning sense of humor?" demanded Millicent suspiciously. She came to the side of the bed. "Let's see your throat." She laid a hand on Eudora's head to tilt it back. "There's a lot of strep—"

"Ow!" winced Eudora.

Millicent took her hand swiftly away and stared down where it had rested. "What's the matter with your head?"

"If I tell you, will you go away?"

"If you want me to," said Millicent stiffly, but remained rooted, her eyes bulging with curiosity.

"I got hit."

"Eudora!" Millicent backed one step and fell into a wicker rocker, which squeaked. Then her small chin quivered. "This is terrible. How did it happen?"

Eudora lay down. "Go away."

The rocker squeaked again. "I'll get you an aspirin."

Eudora watched Millicent as she crossed the room to the white metal medicine chest above the washbasin. She brought Eudora two aspirins in the palm of her tiny hand, and a glass of water. "Now tell me!"

Eudora handed her the glass and a dark look. "Outside the prop roob. Sobeone phoned here and left me a fake bessage to beet him."

"Oh, Eudora. Have you told Lieutenant Tuck? Have you seen a doctor?"

"Dough and yes."

Millicent pattered to the closet and came out with a pair of galoshes, into which she jammed her feet. "He's got to be told," she said, her high voice shaken by excitement. She bundled herself into a tan raincoat, and Eudora watched her with a curiously comforting sense of helplessness. Millicent said, "I'll tell Mrs. Sweetzer you have a cold and she'll send up some breakfast."

"Dot breakfast. Just sobe tobato juice. And you bight take Beg Fife her raincoat. She'll deed it. She'll be at Old College, I think."

Millicent picked up the yellow slicker from where it was drying over the back of a chair. "I'll take care of everything," she said importantly.

Tuck's approach along the hall was heralded by squeals, laughter and slamming doors. There was a tap at her door and then Mrs. Sweetzer opened it. Tuck loomed behind her. "Lieutenant Tuck would like to speak to you, Eudora, if you feel well enough."

"I feel fide," said Eudora darkly.

Mrs. Sweetzer looked as though she would like to stay and hear everything, but Tuck stood smiling patiently down at her so obviously that she bustled out.

Tuck then sat down in the wicker rocker, which creaked

loudly. He fitted his long fingers together into a tent. "Well," he said.

"Well," said Eudora, wondering how many people his vast trench coat could shelter from inclement weather.

"You're very naïve," offered Tuck. "Don't you know that 'Meet me under the old oak tree' is one of the hoariest gags known to the criminal mind?"

"I was blinded with the gleeful idea that you were going to bake a Watson of be," said Eudora.

"Have you tried gargling with hot salt water?"

"I dever humor a code," said Eudora with dignity.

"Well, someone phoned you and said he was me, and you dashed off to meet him. How about particulars?"

"Id the first place, he didn't phode be. I cabe hobe frob Beg Fife's apartment, and the phode bessage was given be by the girl at the desk. Id the second place, I didn't *dash off*. I went to Miss Fitch's for the key, first."

"The key," said Tuck.

"Yes. The bessage said for be to beet you by the outer door of the prop roob, with the key."

"Ho," said Tuck.

"Ho yourself. She wasn't hobe, so I walked to Old College to tell you I couldn't get the key. But before I could oped by bouth, you hit me on the head."

"Miss York," said Tuck. "Do you know anything that you don't know you know, but that someone else knows you know and doesn't want you to tell to the police?"

"I don't dough."

"Good. That's an old gag, too. Somohow, I've never run into a corpse that was a corpse because it knew something that it didn't know it knew but that someone else—"

"Don't go through that agaid—I got it the first time."

"All right. So we have two choices. Either the person who hit you wanted to hit you, and asked for you to bring the key to provide a reason for the rendezvous, should you have felt cagey about going to such a lonely spot, or else he wanted that key to the prop room pretty badly and didn't want to get it himself. That would suggest that the murderer left something behind him which he would like very much to have."

"That's right! I didn't think of that!"

"I wish you had got the key. Because what he wanted would now be missing. And we have all the fingerprints, and a very complete set of photographs of the scene of the crime."

"I don't think your photographs would help you much, dot id that junk shop. Because if I had got the key, and the ban who hit me had reboved whatever he wanted, it still bight have been behind sobething or id sobething, or otherwise idvisible to the cabera."

"Did he come up behind you?" Tuck asked.

"Yes."

"So you didn't catch even a glimpse of what he looked like."

"Dot a glimpse."

"Do you have any idea what he hit you with?"

"Just that it was very, very heavy."

"Let's see the head."

She bobbed her head forward and he looked at her bump. "Has a doctor seen this?"

"Yes. You see, I waited until sobeone came past, and finally Oliver Clarey did, so he phoned for an abbulance."

Tuck looked at her for several seconds. "Let me get the full, rich impact of this. Are you telling me that you lay there in the rain *waiting for someone?*"

"Certainly. I didn't dough how badly I was hurt. You shouldn't walk aroud with a fracture, you dough."

Tuck towered to his feet. "I salute you," he said gravely. He walked to the door and turned. "You clever women are really beyond me. You're not quite human. Will the girl who took the phone message be at the desk now?"

"Yes."

"Good-by. You've been lucky, I think, Miss York."

The door closed after Tuck, and she felt herself relax. *Maybe it was the key that was wanted—not me, but the key.* She closed her eyes, and immediately Ames leaned toward her and said, *"Someday I'll kill you."*

Chapter Fourteen: THE FIEND

THE GIRL AT the desk was a young blonde, very anxious to please. She had not thrown away the phone message she had taken down for Eudora, and Tuck looked at schoolgirl handwriting which had very nearly sent a young woman to her death. "What time was it when this man called?" he asked her.

"Well—it was—did you say you were Lieutenant Tuck?"

"Yes."

She looked at him accusingly out of large blue eyes. "It wasn't *you.*"

"No. What sort of a voice was it?"

She thought. "It was a soft voice," she said at last. "Look, did or did not someone attack Eudora York?"

"Attack?"

She became very pink but repeated significantly, "Attack."

Tuck backed toward the door. "Oh, no. He didn't *attack* her. That is, not in the sense you mean."

"Then what goes on?"

"Something very, very unpleasant. A soft voice, you said? Could it have been a woman's voice?"

"No, at least, I don't think so. Just a soft voice." She suddenly beamed at him. "Very malignant!"

Tuck walked toward the Old College wondering if it had been the same soft voice that had phoned Jim Laird to tell him that his wife was dead. . . .

"Froody," said Tuck, "I don't like this Fiend-in-Human-Shape stuff."

Froody did not reply. His elbow was on the extreme edge of Tuck's desk, his cheek was in his hand, and he was asleep. Tuck reached across the width of the desk and poked him. With a start and a snort Froody was guiltily and volubly awake. "Exactly," he said hurriedly. "I absolutely agree." He tried to look intently at Tuck, with eyes squeezed almost shut against the white glare of the ceiling lights. Tuck looked at his watch. It was 8:30, which was early for Froody's evening languor.

"Froody," said Tuck, "we need about a quart of coffee."

Froody sighed and stood up. "I know what that means. I go down to the drugstore and get a carton of coffee and it leaks on my suit." He rose, picked up the bill Tuck laid on the desk, and went toward the outer office of the Homicide Squad. There was an absurd dignity to his waddle, and from the rear, as always, he made Tuck think of both Queen Victoria and the Dormouse.

Smiling, Tuck began to list the questions which demanded answers if he was ever to learn why Ann Laird died and who killed her. This method was the equivalent of a mental housecleaning. With all obscurities neatly listed in his square black handwriting in his small black notebook, his brain could think again:

1. Why was Ann Laird killed by a blow on the back of the head?

2. Why was she killed in the prop room?

3. Why was her body moved after death?

4. Why did the man with the soft voice telephone Jim Laird?

5. Why did someone attach a mortuary ad to Ann Laird's picture?

6. Why did someone telephone Eudora York and make an appointment, in my name, for a meeting outside the prop room?

7. Why did someone hit her on the head?

8. Why had this blow been so light as to cause very little injury?

9. Does the theory that the murderer is not sane provide answers to the above questions?

10. If so, did any of the incidents occur in order to force the conclusion of insanity?

Tuck had just decided that his mind was fairly free of cobwebs when Froody came in with a round white carton of coffee. He set it on the desk, took a handkerchief from his breast pocket and dabbed at a trickle running down the front of his coat. "I knew it would," he said sadly.

Putting away the handkerchief, he went to the water cooler in the corner and came back with two paper cups, which he filled. Tuck gulped down the contents of his and refilled it. Then he passed the black notebook to Froody, who slowly absorbed both coffee and questions and then said, "You've left out two questions. What was Laird hit with? And what was York hit with?"

"I know what York was hit with," said Tuck. "I went to Old College this morning and I found a couple of mill ends—two-by-fours. They were half hidden in the bushes that grow beside that outer door to the prop room. On a hunch, I talked to Joe, the kid in charge of props, and he told me that on Thursday he'd carried those two mill ends out of the prop room with some laths and some longer pieces he was going to use to brace the balcony. Then he decided these two pieces were too short and chucked them into the bushes. I toted them down here; there were no fingerprints. But the doctor who examined York at the Receiving Hospital says one of those very probably was used to hit her."

"How about Laird? Could one of 'em have been used on her too?"

"The medical examiner says no. Now why was Laird killed by a blow on the back of the head?"

"Someone crept up behind her," said Froody sagely.

"You're sharp tonight."

"Well, he certainly didn't say, 'Turn around, dearie, while I bust open your head!' And we know he crept up behind York, because she says so."

"Which makes it look as though the same person hit both ladies."

Froody's eyes got wide. "Why, sure! What else?"

"I'm just trying out all the possibilities. All right. We still don't know why Laird was hit. With regard to York, there are two angles. Either she was hit to get the key, or the key was only mentioned to suggest a reason for the meeting with me, in that particular place."

"But why drag in the key? I mean, there were a lotta other reasons he could 'a given. I think he wanted the key."

"And yet that's so senseless. Because if someone really wanted something in that prop room, there are two windows, small and high, but easy to break. Instead, we get this elaborate device of phoning York, leaving my name, and hitting her on the head."

"Yeah," said Froody. "Yeah."

"So then we come to the question: 'Why was Laird killed in the prop room?'"

"Because the murderer knew she'd be there, and it was a lonely place, so if she screamed no one would hear."

"Or the murderer could have seen her go in. Remember, she had to go out the front of the building and around to the side. But why was her body moved after death? If she was hit on the back of the head, she'd have fallen forward."

"Sure! But the murderer wanted it to look like she fell and hit her head on that dumbbell."

"Then why did the murderer turn out the light?"

Froody deflated. "Yeah, there's that, of course."

"And here's a honey. Why did the man with the soft voice phone Jim Laird?"

"To tell him his wife was dead. And why tell him his wife was dead? You see, it keeps coming back to a queer sort of gent."

"It certainly does. And something else points in the same direction. Why that coffin ad? Froody, did you track down the newspaper it appeared in?"

"Yeah. It ran for three days, Friday, Saturday, and Sunday, in most papers. No way of finding who bought a paper Friday morning. There's a drugstore just before you get to that big brick gateway to the campus, and they keep their papers out front, in one of those racks where you put in a nickel if you're honest and pull out a paper."

"And so someone pulled out a paper and tore out that ad and stuck it with chewing gum to the bulletin board. And up pops the good old Fiend again."

"I don't see what you've got against the Fiend," said Froody earnestly. "It's the only way you can get an explanation for some of this stuff that's happened."

"And that's exactly what I object to. It's too darned easy. What you wind up doing is blaming everything that's happened onto a convenient lunatic. 'Why was Laird killed?' A lunatic at large. But that doesn't explain anything. Because a lunatic has to have a reason for killing. It may be an abnormal reason, but even the 'homicidal maniac' of song and story has some perverted reason, real to him. So even if we adopt this lunatic theory, we come right back to where we started from. Why was Ann Laird killed?"

"If we don't adopt the lunatic theory, what do we adopt?"

"I've been wondering whether some of the unexplained facets of this affair couldn't be accounted for with the idea that the murderer wants us to think that a madman is at work." He laughed. "But that really doesn't help much. Because then you replace a lunatic with a sane man who tries to make us think he isn't sane by (a) adopt-

ing a 'nasty' tone and phoning the dead girl's husband;
(b) sticking a coffin to the dead girl's picture; (c) adopt-
ing a 'malignant' voice and luring another girl to a lonely
spot, where (d) he hits her on the head. And how sane
is 'sane' and who behaves like a lunatic?"

"It looks to me," Froody observed, "like you're being
a complete acrostic. You don't believe anything. You don't
believe in a lunatic, and you don't believe in a sane man
pretending to be a lunatic, so what do you believe?"

"I believe that Laird was killed for a plain, simple reason. I believe that York was hit in order to get the key to
the prop room, because our plain and simple murderer
had left evidence behind him. Why he didn't break a window, I don't know, but I'd rather look for a reason for that
than grab at the Fiend."

"How about the phone call to Laird? How about the
coffin?"

"You know," said Tuck, "I'm wondering if someone
else—someone who was glad Ann Laird was dead, viciously
glad, if you please—didn't gloat to the husband and didn't
make a joke with the coffin ad."

"But then he's nuts!" said Froody.

Tuck shook his head. "Just uninhibited, shall we say?
At any rate, I'm avoiding the Fiend like the devil until
there's reason to believe in him; some clear picture of a
madman's motive."

The telephone on Tuck's desk rang. He put the receiver to his ear, his eye on Froody, who was drinking another paper cup of coffee. "Tuck speaking."

A woman's voice, speaking distinctly, yet undertoned
with fright: "This is Meg Fife. Someone just tried to kill
me. He came up behind me and hit me on the head."

The Administration Building loomed huge against a
night sky of low clouds and was desolate in the steady drip
of rain. Tuck and Froody and Meg Fife stood on the side-

walk, looking toward the long arcade along the front of
the building, connecting the left wing with the right.
Pallid yellow light spilled out from each arch.

"The phone booths are there, in the left wing," explained
Meg, the fright still in her voice. "I came along
the sidewalk to that middle walk to the main door, and
then I turned left inside the arcade."

Tuck started toward the scene of the third crime, and
Froody and Meg followed. Inside the arcade he turned
left as Meg had done—he noticed that their footsteps on
the reddish tiles made echoes. The wide doors to the left
wing were open, and directly beyond them were four
empty phone booths. Meg walked ahead, her yellow
slicker rustling stiffly, and when she reached the end
phone booth, stopped and looked at them over her
shoulder. "I was in this one. I looked up my number and
found a nickel. I had just taken the receiver from the
hook when something hit me on the head. I came to with
my forehead leaning against the mouthpiece of the telephone. So I picked up the nickel from the floor and phoned
you. Then I made my other call and went home, where
I waited until you came."

Tuck went to a stone bench just opposite the last arch.
"Sit down," he suggested. "You look very shaky."

"I feel shaky." Meg's laugh was forced. She sat down in
one corner of the bench, looking up at them like a child.
Raindrops sparkled in her fine, loose hair. Froody sat down
in the other corner of the bench.

Tuck stood in front of Meg. "What happened just before
you were hit?"

"Well, I had dinner with a friend who came to town
unexpectedly. We ate downtown. I got off the streetcar
at eight-thirty. The chimes were ringing."

"Wait a minute," Tuck commanded. "Miss York told me
there were to be four performances of the play. I assumed
the last two would be on Monday and Tuesday nights."

Meg shook her head. "No. They will be on next Friday and Saturday. Theoretically, week-night performances would interfere with the students' outside work."

"I see. Go on."

"So after I got off the streetcar, I went straight along University toward my apartment, which as you know is near the far end of campus. When I reached this building, I decided to make my phone call from here—I had promised to call at eight-thirty, and thought I'd be on the dot. It was a business call, to the talent scout who is arranging for my screen test. So I came down that middle walk, as we did just now, down this arcade to the telephones, and the rest you know."

"Let's see where he hit you."

Meg obediently tilted her head and raised the right cascade of hair. Tuck looked closely and saw a faint red bruise behind her right ear. He straightened, and Meg, letting the hair drop back into place, again looked up.

"Did you meet anyone on your walk from the streetcar?"

"No. That is, a man walked toward me just as I passed the drugstore. He was coming from campus. We exchanged a glance from under our umbrellas; I caught just a glimpse. It was no one I know."

"You're sure of that?"

"Well, it was no one I know well. But we were right under those ghastly yellow lamps that light the short block just before you get to the gateway to campus—"

"Which," finished Tuck, "turn your lips purple and your skin livid, and in general seem calculated to make a mother look at her only child, providing she's able to recognize him, with disgust."

"Exactly. So all I can say is, he was someone I don't know well. Whether he was someone I've never seen in my life, I can't say."

"What did he look like?"

"A fiend from hell." Meg grinned wanly. "His umbrella was tipped back, because the rain was slanting from the south, and the light fell right on his face. So the best description I can give you is that he is a man of middle height, with saffron skin, lips the color of raw liver, and glittering eyes. Oh, and he had on a dark suit, and no hat."

"So you and this man passed each other like ships in the night, and you went through the gates of campus and along University to this building. Did you at any time have the sensation of being followed?"

Meg hesitated. "Well, you know that wooded place between Old College and this building?"

"Yes, indeed."

"When I was passing that, I hurried. You see, Oliver Clarey told me today what happened to Eudora there last night. I wasn't actually frightened, but—I hurried. And I looked back. A man was coming from the foot of campus. He didn't seem to be following me, exactly. He had a big umbrella tilted down in front of his face."

"And what did he look like?"

"He was more of a silhouette than anything else."

"I see. And then you made for the phones?"

"Yes."

Tuck looked down the arcade. "No one came along here, that's certain. The echoes are magnificent." He turned and looked at the arch opposite the bench.

Froody stood up and waddled out into the night. In a moment he reappeared, around the corner of the last arch. With infinite caution, he tiptoed through the arch, across the hall of the left wing; flattening himself against the phone booths, he came to the last booth from which Meg had phoned, where he raised his short arm and came down with an imaginary weapon on an imaginary head. Then he faced them. "That's how he did it."

Tuck looked down at Meg. "The door of the booth was open, of course."

"Oh, yes. No reason to close it—no one was about."

"Except," said Froody, with a bland look at Tuck, "the Fiend in Human Shape."

"Do you know why someone would want to hit you on the head?" Tuck asked Meg, rather hopelessly.

"Oh, yes," she replied in a calm voice.

Froody walked closer, and Tuck straightened.

"I think," said Meg, "that I was hit by someone who doesn't like Juliet."

"Someone Who Doesn't Like Juliet," echoed Tuck, his mind making capitals.

"I have only the layman's knowledge of lunacy, of course, but I sincerely believe I was struck by the same hatred that killed Ann Laird and tried to kill Eudora. I believe a lunatic is loose whose delusion, or fixation, or whatever you call it, involves not only woman-hatred, but woman-hatred centered on the Juliet character."

"But Eudora York didn't play Juliet!"

"No. But she had on this slicker when she was hit, Mr. Tuck. Oliver told me so. A good many people know this slicker belongs to me. And as you can see, it's pretty unmistakable. I played Juliet, Mr. Tuck, and so did Ann Laird."

"No," said Tuck, turning his eyes to heaven. "It's too much."

Meg shrugged. "I don't ask that *you* believe it. *I* do." She stood up. "I'd like to go home now."

As they rode in Tuck's black sedan toward Meg's apartment house, she said suddenly, "Look. Professor Brewer lives just down the hall from me. Why don't you ask him about my idea?"

"I will," said Tuck grimly.

Professor Brewer looked a little surprised at the soggy delegation lined up before his door. "Come in," he invited. "You look as though you might be on the edge of collapse, Miss Fife. Anything wrong?"

"I've had a rather narrow escape," she said. "Mr. Tuck will tell you about it."

Brewer focused his brilliant eyes on Tuck.

"I want to ask you one question, Professor. In your opinion, could there possibly be such a thing as a lunatic with a delusion built around a hatred of Juliet?"

"Juliet?" frowned Brewer.

"Juliet Shakespeare," offered Froody.

Brewer smiled and sobered. "Sit down," he said. "Let's go a little further into this."

Brewer sat at his desk, his plump hands resting quietly in the pool of light pouring down from the desk lamp. "You're thinking of Ann Laird, of course."

"It's gone a little further than that," Tuck said. "Last night Miss York was hit on the head. Tonight, Miss Fife was hit on the head. Miss Fife, as you probably know, took over Mrs. Laird's part."

"Yes," said Brewer.

"And Miss York was wearing this raincoat when she was struck," Meg said earnestly, her hand touching the yellow slicker.

Brewer's face lightened. "I see what you mean. Two Juliets, one girl mistaken for Juliet, and all of them hit on the head."

"Yes," said Tuck. "What I want to know is whether this supposititious lunatic could be impelled by his delusion to injure a woman simply because she played the part of Juliet. Is that possible?"

Brewer considered his hands for a moment and then looked steadily at Tuck. "Yes," he said. "It's possible."

Tuck looked back emptily.

"There would be a paranoic trend to the lunacy, and an elaborate persecutory delusion. But it's quite possible." Brewer grinned pleasantly. "In fact, I could show you case histories of paranoics and paranoic schizophrenics which would make the delusion you mention seem simple and rather pretty."

Chapter Fifteen: THAT WAY MADNESS LIES

EUDORA trudged up the steps of Old College, unconscious of the sunny morning. Her dark brown skirt and sweater exactly fitted her mood. She reached the porch; facing her was the bulletin board, with Ann Laird's picture replaced by one of Meg Fife. She wished dully that she could manage as neat a job of replacement in her own heart, and wishing that, admitted for the first time that all the old attraction she had felt for Ames was renascent. Her unruly fears about him had served to bring him again into her conscious mind, where he swaggered and frightened her.

Three girls were giggling in the far corner of the porch; they looked absurdly young to her, snatching their moment of silliness before the first bell dragged them to nine-o'clock class. She heard feet ascending the steps behind her and glanced over her shoulder at Professor Brewer, a briefcase in one hand and a smile on his face.

"Well, Miss York," he said, "you seem to have hit the nail on the head. I don't know how you did it, but I have to admit your paranoic theory has been somewhat confirmed."

"What?"

"And my pathological interior now bows himself out."

"What?"

"You don't know yet, I see. Miss Fife was hit on the head last night. She's possessed by the imaginative notion that Ann Laird and you and she were all the victims of a lunatic who doesn't like Juliet. You were wearing her slicker, you see, and so you were mistaken for her, or rather for Juliet. Such an elaborate delusion as that would belong to a paranoic, most probably."

For a long minute Eudora couldn't speak. Professor Brewer turned to go. She grabbed his sleeve. "But is it possible? Is such a delusion possible?"

"What do you think, as a student of Abnormal Psychology?"

"Well, it's certainly no more far-fetched than Wagner's idea that he had been placed on earth by God to rid Illinois of the human race."

"Exactly. What we don't know about paranoia, of course, makes an adequate decision rather difficult. But my reaction was very much like yours just now. So many case histories occurred to me which were no more strange, that I was forced to tell Mr. Tuck that Miss Fife's theory certainly couldn't be brushed aside as fantastic."

Eudora felt suddenly warm toward Professor Brewer.

"And it *does* explain so much, doesn't it? It explains why Ann was killed, for one thing."

"Yes. Yes, it does." He looked at his watch and then hurried into the building. The first bell rang.

The giggling girls stopped giggling and straggled toward Eudora, who was still standing beside the bulletin board. She smiled into their pretty faces and noticed for the first time how good it was to see the sun again.

Of one thing she was sure. Ames was no paranoic with a hatred for Juliet. In all the time they had spent together, she knew that such a delusion would have shown itself to her.

"All I know," said the girl at the desk, "is that Eudora usually comes in about this time. If you care to, you may wait in the lounge."

"Thank you," Tuck said, and turned toward the archway leading into the large dark room where swains awaited their girls. The lounge was a big room furnished with lavish use of plush, and a grand piano. It was entirely empty. He had not been waiting long when Eudora came through the archway. She was smiling. As she approached him, she opened the newspaper that was tucked under her arm, and spread it wide so he could see the front page.

JULIET KILLER STRIKES AGAIN! said the headline of a half-column story topped by an excellent photograph of Meg Fife.

"Where did the reporters get the story?" Tuck asked. "I didn't tell 'em. Froody didn't."

"But Meg did," said Eudora.

"Or her talent scout. She phoned him right after the attack."

"Or the talent scout," agreed Eudora. "Publicity."

Tuck held his long head briefly in his hands and then spoke quietly. "I am used to simple crimes, Miss York. Murders in haste, usually in the presence of witnesses. Or a body, very stale, which little boys find in some bushes. The last murder I investigated involved two men of low intellect, one of whom cut open the other's abdomen with a razor in a bar. The motive was simple—money which was owed him had not been paid."

"You're certainly getting variety," offered Eudora.

Tuck looked at her solemnly. "All lettuces have hearts. All men have hearts. Therefore all men are lettuce."

"I beg your pardon?" said Eudora.

"Miss York, one thing annoys me. Circumstances which can apparently mean only one thing have clamped themselves onto me like handcuffs. I have become the prisoner of one obsessive thought: 'Who is this person who doesn't like Juliet?' I don't like that, Miss York. I don't like it because I know how easy it is to read a logical relationship into events. That doesn't mean that the logical relationship exists. I have never proved to my satisfaction that there wasn't a reasonable motive, one not involving lunacy, for killing Ann Laird. Before I could satisfy myself on that score, except in a most cursory way, along you come with your paranoic theory. Before I satisfied myself as to the probability of that, along comes the attack on you, and the attack on Miss Fife, and that blasted yellow raincoat, and lo, apparently the paranoic theory is richly confirmed. *But only apparently.* There is no evidence to substantiate the idea that a paranoic is at work except a sketchily induced relationship between the three crimes. And I don't like it. I don't like it at all."

"Did you come here to mourn?" asked Eudora.

"I came here on a very thin hope. *Did* you have on that yellow slicker when you were hit?"

"I did."

"You seem very pleased about something."

"Don't forget that the paranoic angle was my baby."

"I'm not apt to."

"Remember when I told you about someone starting the rumor that Ann voted for herself? And do you know someone voted against Meg playing Juliet?"

"I do. And may I add that I'm unimpressed."

"With those two little events, you have two deviations from normal. Whoever started the rumor about Ann didn't like Ann. Whoever voted against continuing the performance didn't like Meg Fife. I'd like to know who that person is."

Tuck rose and began to walk up and down. "I'll admit that the rumor about Ann must have been started by someone who didn't like Ann. But the person who voted against ringing up the curtain didn't necessarily dislike Meg. You're taking the historical viewpoint, I'm afraid. Knowing that her performance as Juliet netted Meg a screen test, you're deciding that whoever voted against going on with the show did so to spite Meg. Whereas actually there was no way of guessing at the time the vote was taken that the performance would have such happy results for Meg. So it's much more logical, on the basis of what was known when the vote was taken, to suppose that the one person who voted against the show going on did so out of fondness for Ann rather than dislike of Meg. And that would mean two people to look for, rather than one. One who hated Ann Laird and one who liked her." .

"I'm going to find out who they are," said Eudora.

Tuck stood up. "I can see the headlines now. 'Brilliant Woman Psychologist Traps Murderer.'" He grinned.

"You think I'm silly. You think my idea that there's a connection between a mean little rumor and an odd vote and a murder is silly. Don't you?"

"Well," said Tuck, "yes."

"Why? Why couldn't it have been the murderer who started the rumor that Ann Laird voted for herself?"

"The person who started the tale is a petty person. And a petty person is less likely to murder with violence than almost any other person I can think of."

"But it's not impossible. And has it occurred to you that maybe the person who voted against ringing up the curtain did so because his nerves wouldn't stand the idea of going through with the same lines he had spoken when Ann was on stage?"

"An agreeable sense of delicacy, which leaves the coffin ad unexplained, since we had already decided that gesture involved a cold and malignant sense of humor."

"Oh, you make me sick," snapped Eudora.

"No. What makes you sick is my regrettable lack of enthusiasm, plus a certain modest ability to see both sides of the coin."

"This coin," said Eudora with great sweetness, "seems to have three sides, doesn't it? Ann, Meg and me. Maybe that's why you're a little dizzy." .

"All coins have two sides. This has three sides. Therefore, this is not a coin," said Tuck gravely. "Did you know, Miss York, that I have a great respect for coins? They cut so many Gordian knots. You flip a coin, and by that simple gesture summon up chance to your aid. And chance is more potent than most people believe. I have traced back great events, and found that they sprouted from some infinitesimal accident. Chance, the first cause, Good-by."

He was quite aware of Eudora's blank stare at his abrupt departure, but he suddenly had to get out of that large dim room. He stood quite still on the sunny, flagstoned terrace of the dormitory, staring at the opulent white clouds floating above the far hills of Hollywood.

It was entirely a matter of chance that Meg Fife was hit on the head. No one could have planned to hit her, because no one could have known that at eight-thirty she would walk along campus and make that phone call. Someone happened to see her pass, in her yellow slicker. . . .

Eudora, after a disgruntled look at Tuck's retreating back, drifted into the small office where the mailboxes were, hoping idly for a letter from home. The girl at the desk asked, "Have you seen it?" and pointed up at a new bulletin on the board above her head.

"Mrs. Sweetzer's in a cold sweat," the girl went on. "She sees a homicidal maniac behind every bush. In a few days she'll probably have an armored car to take us back and forth from the library."

The phone rang and she answered it while Eudora quickly scanned the bulletin.

"Pretend," said a voice behind her, "that it's addressed to you." Tuck was looking down at her with an odd blend of jubilation and concern on his face.

"What do you mean?" she asked.

He took her arm and piloted her into the lounge, speaking in a low voice. "I know why Meg Fife was hit. I know why she wasn't killed. I know why you were hit. And I want you to be very careful. Because I'm afraid an old gag comes into the picture. You know something that you don't know the importance of, and someone else knows you know it, and doesn't like it at all."

Eudora stood speechless, looking up at him.

"I've found the error in my reasoning, I think. You see, you weren't hit because you were mistaken for Meg Fife; she was hit because she was mistaken for you!"

Chapter Sixteen: THE BALLOT

TUCK AT LAST found Professor Brewer in one of the library cubicles, where professors retired to escape interruption and to work on whatever they might be writing as a contribution to their field of endeavor, and as an additional bulwark to their status with the university.

Brewer at first paid no attention to his knock, but when Tuck called his name, Brewer opened the door and offered him a chair. Tuck said abruptly, "Professor Brewer, I know that the psychoanalysis of a patient takes hundreds of hours. But I'm wondering if a trained psychologist like yourself could determine in a general way, and in a few hours, whether a person was sane or not."

A look of caution came over Brewer's face. "Well . . ."

"I'm thinking of paranoia," said Tuck. "Or some equally serious abnormality."

"And are you thinking also of our gentleman who doesn't like Juliet?" asked Brewer.

"No. Frankly, I've deserted that idea. But I have not deserted the notion that the killer may be crazy. I don't think Ann Laird was killed because she was Juliet. But she may have been killed by a psychopath of some sort—maybe one of the people who knew she was going down to the prop room."

"A good many people knew that. I was present at that dress rehearsal, and in addition to the cast and the people backstage, more than a dozen people were scattered about the theater watching the show."

"Well," said Tuck, "I always work on probables first. Saves time. And it seems probable to me that the people

closest to the girl—I don't mean physically, you understand—would most likely have a motive for killing her,
even though it might be an insane motive."

"You're right there."

"If I gave you a list of these students, could you find
out whether one of them belongs in an asylum?"

"I can only say this. If a person were mentally abnormal, that abnormality would possibly reveal itself to me
in a short space of time. There would be the IQ, of course,
from which we couldn't expect to learn much, since the
student would have at least a normal intelligence in order to pass the entrance exams when he entered college.
I could also give a mental stability test. I could take an
encephalogram, which would reveal a markedly abnormal
brain wave. Epilepsy, for example, has its characteristic
wave. I could also question the student briefly about his
past life, his health, his opinions. I should say that in an
hour and a half or two hours, I could discover any marked
deviation from normal."

"Will you do this?" Tuck asked.

Professor Brewer looked at the mass of papers on his
desk. Then he looked at Tuck. "Certainly," he said. "Glad
to. But if these students knew that they were being questioned as suspects in a murder case, and worse than that,
if they knew their sanity was being questioned, some
would undoubtedly tell their families, and I think we
could count on at least one indignant letter finding its way
to the President's desk. I would be in the soup."

"Lie," said Tuck calmly. "Make up some story they'll
swallow."

Brewer's eyes went again to the papers on his desk. "In
my book," he said, smiling, "there is a chapter on the
artistically endowed. Aren't most of the people you want
me to question in Drama?"

"All of 'em," said Tuck, and reaching into his inner
breast pocket, he laid a neatly written list on Brewer's

desk. There were five names: *Oliver Clarey, Paul Ober, Meg Fife, Dave Draska, Eudora York.*

"Eudora York!" exclaimed Brewer. "You don't think—"

"No. I don't think so. But I want to know." He rose, with an upward glance at the low ceiling which his head cleared by inches.

Professor Brewer stood up too and opened the door. "I'll figure out a way to handle this tactfully. I'll let you know as soon as I find anything definite."

"Thank you, Professor Brewer. I know how valuable your time is, and I deeply appreciate your help."

"Don't mention it. I expect to find it interesting."

I hope you do, thought Tuck, as he walked down the long and silent corridor outside the numbered cubicles.

"No," said the housekeeper's voice. "Mr. Ames isn't home."

"Do you know where he is? This is Eudora York."

"Oh, Miss York," said the housekeeper. "He'll be sorry to have missed you. He's gone fishing. He left Thursday night, in his own car. I haven't the slightest idea what you can fish for at night, but that's Mr. Ames."

"Yes," echoed Eudora. "That's Ames. Thank you." She slowly replaced the receiver and looked out the window at the library, across the street. Gone fishing. *I'll go to the library and do some reading for that paper that's due,* she told herself desperately.

But sitting in the long oak-paneled room, at a long oak table, she was unable to concentrate on the page before her. The intense silence of the study hall was a conspirator with her darkest imaginings, and as her eyes went from bent head to bent head, her thoughts talked together.

Tuck's reasoning is absolutely valid, of course. Because I wore the yellow slicker first. So the person who hit me would naturally assume it was my slicker. So he thought Meg was me when he saw her in the rain the next night.

That seems much more logical in view of the meeting the murderer arranged with me, and also because there could have been no forethought about the attack on Meg.

But why would someone want to kill me?

She resolutely ignored the reply which was as glaring as neon letters inside her head, and grabbed at a straw.

Maybe Tuck's right. Maybe I know something dangerous to the murderer. Maybe I know why Ann was killed, only haven't fitted the pieces together.

She tried fitting pieces together: *Let's see. If Ann Laird wasn't killed because she was Juliet, she was killed because she was Ann Laird. And that takes me back to the people who knew her best, since even if a twisted mind is at work, that person probably knew Ann. And the killer was probably in the theater when she announced she was going to the prop room.*

Jim Laird. Meg Fife. Professor Romaine. Oliver Clarey. Dave Draska. Paul Ober. And Millie. And Professor Brewer.

Jim Laird? He couldn't have stuck the coffin to the bulletin board. He couldn't have phoned himself. Could he be insane? Behind that mild face, was there a mind gone bad? The possibility that Laird was insane lacked conviction.

Well, Meg Fife. She was older than she looked. Could that first performance of the play have meant a last chance to her? Could she have intended perhaps only to injure Ann to such an extent that Ann would be unable to go on, and could she have struck too hard? And then could she have planned the affair with the yellow slicker as a design to establish her own innocence? *No, that is rather thin. Murderers in books do that, but in real life?* Well, there was a possible motive for Meg, and not too mad a one at that: *Success-worship is a universal disease, and sometimes gnaws the decency out of the worshiper.*

Professor Romaine. Was her famous eccentricity indicative of a deeper oddness? As only part of an iceberg shows, the real danger lying in the great submerged part, could Romaine's delightful individuality be part of an individuality less delightful? What motive, though, even a mad motive? Perhaps something to do with that tragic and unavoidable jealousy that sometimes exists in the heart of an older woman for a younger one. But Romaine showed fondness for Ann, and had given generously of her time and knowledge in building Ann's talent.

Oliver Clarey had been in love with Ann and was almost certainly a neurotic. That tautness, that almost pitiful attempt at a reckless nonchalance. *But he certainly didn't hit me, because he was the one who found me. He came past singing, and had gone past singing at nine o'clock. Or had he?*

Dave Draska. What motive there? If there was one, it was well hidden.

Paul Ober liked Ann. He seemed to like Ann. They were good friends. But why was he such an essentially sad person? What secret unhappiness gave his face that tragic look that was too old for it?

Millie. No, not Millie.

Professor Brewer? What motive? Was he a lecher who made the mistake of leching after a virtuous young matron, and had he rectified his error and saved his reputation by killing her?

It all sounds so wild and woolly, somehow. But then murder is wild, the oldest wildness there is, and someone murdered Ann. Maybe thinking of the possible case history involved will make one of these motives seem more believable. For instance, Ober's imaginary delusion might be built around his shortness, and its effect on a man who wants above all else to succeed as an actor. But a lot of actors are short. Long on courage, probably. Maybe Ober is short on courage.

Male, 21, health fair. Unmarried. Family history negative. Growth somewhat retarded. Mental capacity average. From the age of 17, excessively sensitive about his short stature, with a consistent effort to hide this sensitivity under a pose of calmness and laziness. Was unable to concentrate properly on his studies while in college because of a constant sense of being at a disadvantage, through no fault of his. Engaged heavily in all athletic activities open to him in order to convince himself that he was as good as the other men in his class. At the age of 20, became convinced the world was not treating him right because of his short stature. This sense of persecution focused on a young woman with whom he acted several parts while in a dramatics class. He began to see in certain of her remarks an intention to mock him because of his smallness (which was of course not intended). A physical attraction to this young woman might have intensified the pain of this feeling. At one of the rehearsals of the balcony scene from *Romeo and Juliet*, which he and this young woman played together, began to hate her intensely. Thought the scene served to emphasize his lack of height. This hatred took final form when he followed her to a lonely part of the building and struck her on the head, causing her death. Felt no remorse over this act, but rather a resentment toward the girl for having driven him to it. Memory good. Orientation good.

If I'm not careful, I'll believe he did it. But anyway, my point is proved. My imaginary case against Paul could be written into any textbook as an example of paranoia. And I'll bet any one of my crazy-sounding reasons would make just as good a case history as Paul's did. The only trouble being they're not true. One of them may be, though. But guessing is no good. Her thoughts were interrupted when someone scraped back the chair next to her.

It was Millicent, panting a little under an unusually large load of books. "Hello," she whispered. "Thought I might as well sit next to you."

Seeing Millicent set off another train of thought in Eudora's mind. "Millicent," she whispered back, "who told you that story about Ann voting for herself?"

"Meg," whispered Millicent. "Why?"

"And did you tell Ann?"

"Yes. I thought she should know. Why?"

Eudora stood up. "Just wondered. Gotta go to class now. 'By."

Meg was the first person Eudora saw on entering the theater, where the class in Advanced Drama met for two hours twice a week. She and Draska were arguing quietly in one corner, Draska with many a fluid gesture, Meg with an unblinking immobility. As Eudora came up to them Meg was saying, "—as far as my playing Juliet younger goes, Dave, your Friar Laurence is about thirty years old, and he's written as sixty if a day. So—"

Dave saw Eudora and waved a lackadaisical arm. "We're just catting again, darling," he said.

Meg gave a thin smile. "He's catting. I'm being a lady."

Dave drooped his lids down over his black eyes. "Oh, you're always a lady, Meg. That's your big trouble."

"Meg," asked Eudora, "who told you that Ann voted for herself?"

"That Ann voted for her—oh, that. Lily told me." She turned to Dave and said sweetly, "You told Lily, Dave."

Dave's long fingers curved in and touched his chest. "Me?"

"Yes," said Meg, firmly. "You."

Dave seemed to remember something. "Oh, yes." He looked at Eudora. "You see, I happened to see her vote when I went around collecting them. It dropped to the floor, and when I picked it up it had unfolded. She'd written down her own name."

"I don't believe it," said Meg.

Dave ignored her. "I'll tell you how I happened to mention it, Eudora. Lily came to me with some story about Ann talking me down, and it made me sore, so I said I wouldn't put too much faith in a person who didn't stick too close to Hoyle herself, and then it—just spilled out. I've felt like a rat ever since."

Meg said, "Only Ann didn't talk you down to Lily—because Lily told me what she said. She simply told her in a general way that marriage was a very serious step to take. That was just after you'd planted your fraternity pin on Lily's bosom. And I think that was darned sweet of Ann. Don't you, Eudora?"

"Yes, I do."

"Too, too sweet," said Dave. "And she also had a temper like Katharine the Shrew."

"Not that he wants to speak ill of the dead," said Meg to Eudora.

"Ill of her? I'm doing her a good turn! The way everyone's talking about her, she'll have a reputation as the most saccharine little elf that ever patted dogs on the head. Sure she had a temper. Once she got mad at me and called me a two-cylinder Hamlet. I didn't mind, because I knew she liked me. She didn't bother getting mad at people she didn't like. She ignored 'em."

Now I wonder, thought Eudora. *No—a good many people have quick tempers, but they aren't murdered because of that alone. Wait, though. Maybe Ann lost her temper and lashed out at just the wrong person. A person primed to kill.*

"I don't suppose you still happen to have that vote, do you?" she asked Dave, as he started to walk away.

"No. Why would I?"

"Obviously you couldn't, because it never existed," said Meg.

"Do you have the votes from last Friday?" persisted Eudora.

"You mean when we decided whether or not to ring up?

No, I—wait a minute! Yes! I stuffed 'em into my notebook, and I haven't opened it since, so they should still be there." He opened his notebook and lifted out a wad of ragged slips of paper. "Here they are."

Eudora extended a hand.

"What do you want with 'em?" asked Draska curiously.

Without replying, Eudora sorted them swiftly until she came to one bearing a small *No*. It had been torn from a 5 x 7" notebook, and was unlined. She folded it across its original crease and put it in her purse.

"What do you want that for?" asked Meg.

Eudora was relieved of the necessity of answering by the abrupt and belated entrance of Professor Romaine. She cast them one of her smiles and went down the center aisle, her arms laden with a sizable stack of papers. The chattering stopped.

She set down the papers on the end seat of the first row. "Today," she announced, "we are going to learn our parts in fifteen minutes. I have some splendid scenes here. One is for a man and woman—a love scene done entirely in a series of grunts. Who would like to try it?"

Several arms waved, and Professor Romaine thrust parts at two of them. Meg had already started down the aisle to a seat in the front row, and Eudora followed her, looking to right and left for a 5 x 7" notebook.

"Eudora!" called Professor Romaine. Eudora saw that she was flourishing a part. She went down and took it. "This scene *seems* to belong to the man," said Professor Romaine, "because he has recently cut off a woman's head. You must steal it from him, Eudora. I should, if I were you, manage a magnificent bit of business at exactly the right moment." Then her dark gaze left Eudora and searched the students' faces. "Paul!" she called, waving another side. He strolled down the aisle to take it, glanced over it and then looked straight at Eudora, nodded, and drew his hand across his throat. They went to a far corner of the theater to go over the scene.

The door at the head of the middle aisle opened. Professor Brewer came in, closed it after him and went briskly down to Professor Romaine. They drew apart and conversed quietly.

"We'll cut down to, 'You're very conceited, aren't you,'" Paul was saying, and Eudora stopped wondering what Professor Romaine and Brewer were saying and gave her attention to the task at hand.

But in a very few minutes her curiosity was satisfied.

"May I have your attention?" called Professor Romaine. Heads were raised from parts. "May I present Professor Brewer, of the Psychology Department, who has a request to make of you." She then went to a seat in the front row, where she sat very straight, looking through the opened curtains of the stage at Juliet's balcony.

Professor Brewer sounded both hurried and unctuous. "I am writing a book," he began without preface. "Professors, as you know, have their homework too. In my book is a chapter called 'Youth Creative.' For that chapter, I want to talk to a number of students engaged in some form of creative activity. All of the histories I acquire will not be used, so I cannot promise you even an anonymous immortality in return for your help. I have chosen several names from this class, because these students have exhibited an unusual degree of creative activity. If these students will come to my office, Room 208 of this building, I would like to arrange for interviews at their convenience." He looked down at a slip of paper in his hand. "Oliver Clarey."

Eudora looked at the back of Oliver's dark head. It turned toward the student next to him. He seemed to be smiling.

"Paul Ober."

Paul looked at Eudora, and then down at his part. He was also smiling.

"Meg Fife."

Meg looked quickly up from the part she had been studying. She stared rigidly at Brewer for a moment.

"Dave Draska."

Dave shrugged carelessly.

"Eudora York."

Eudora jumped. Brewer caught her eye and grinned. Then he put the list away in the side pocket of his coat and said, "Thank you, Professor Romaine—," and looking around the room—"I'll expect you after class. Please don't fail me." With a nod at Professor Romaine, he went up the aisle as hurriedly as he had gone down.

"You didn't expect to hear your name, did you?" asked Paul.

She turned toward him and saw him looking at her out of those huge clear eyes.

"Do you want me to do the introduction?" asked Paul, as they walked together down the side aisle toward the steps leading past the footlights to the stage.

"Please," she begged. "I'll get the table and chairs in place. I'll do that better, I think."

While she moved the prompter's table to the center of the stage, Paul leaned against the proscenium arch and announced in that easy voice of his, "The play is Emlyn Williams' *Night Must Fall.* The scene is a cottage in a lonely wood in England. The characters are Dan and Olivia. Olivia is a frustrated intellectual who hates her job as companion to her cross old aunt. Dan, by being very charming and boyish, has buttered up the old lady, and has left his job at the big nearby resort hotel in order to push her wheelchair. Olivia does not like Dan, and does not believe he is the cheerful, normal lad he pretends to be. There has been a tragedy in the neighborhood: a rich and gay lady has disappeared from the hotel, and the police are beginning to comb the surroundings for her body."

"Oooo!" said a girl's voice in the audience.

A smile came into Paul's tone. "They haven't found it—yet." He went to the wing, picked up a stick of wood from the floor, cut down the lights, and sat opposite Eudora at the table. Deliberately, he took a clasp-knife from his pocket, opened it, and began to whittle. Eudora read her first line from the script spread out on the table in front of her:

OLIVIA: You're very conceited, aren't you?
DAN: Yes. . . .
OLIVIA: And you *are* acting all the time, aren't you?
DAN: Actin'? Actin' what?

(Paul leaned suddenly across the table and stared into her eyes. It was strange, seeing his eyes so close. The green-gray iris was circled with a thin rim of blue; she could see her own face reflected in the pupil.) Look at the way I can look you in the eyes. I'll stare you out. . . .

(Eudora drew back a little. With a laugh, Paul dropped back into his chair. She remembered to look down for her next line.)

OLIVIA: I have a theory it's the criminals who *can* look you in the eyes, and the honest people who blush and look away.
DAN: Oh. . . .

(Smiling, Paul began to whittle again.)

OLIVIA (challenging): It's a very blank look, though, isn't it?
DAN: Is it?

(Eudora leaned forward, forcing his eyes to hers. It was an insolent stare that he gave her. But she saw a muscle twitch, once, beside his mouth.)

OLIVIA: You *are* acting, aren't you?

(The insolent stare dropped to the knife, and then returned.)

DAN (*in a whisper, almost joyfully*): Yes!
OLIVIA: *And what are you like when you stop acting?*
DAN: *I dunno, it's so long since I stopped.*
OLIVIA: *But when you're alone?*

(Paul's hand stopped, and then drew a deliberate curl of wood from the stick.)

DAN: Then I act more than ever I do.

OLIVIA: Why?

DAN: I dunno; 'cause I like it. . . .

(Paul stood up and swung himself to the table, his back three-quarters to the audience.)

Now what d'ye say if I ask a question or two for a change? Just for a change. . . . Why can't you take an interest in some other body but me?

OLIVIA: I'm not interested in you. Only you don't talk. That's bound to make people wonder.

(A slow, merry smile spread and spread on Paul's face. He gave her an outrageous wink.)

DAN: I can talk a lot sometimes. A drop o' drink makes a power o' difference to me. You'd be surprised. . . .

OLIVIA: I wonder if I would. . . .

DAN: I know you would. . . .

OLIVIA: I think I can diagnose you, all right.

(A slow, shrewd look came over Paul's face, making it much older and brassy-hard. Then it smoothed away, and he was handsome again.)

DAN: Carry on.

OLIVIA: You haven't any feelings—at all . . .

(And then it happened. Somehow the scene jogged into reality, or perhaps Paul merged into Dan. The face looking down into hers was certainly that of a stranger. She realized that the knife was stone-still on the strip of wood, and she realized that Paul Ober had stopped breathing. She didn't have to look at the lines to go on.)

But you live in a world of your own—a world of your own imagination. . . .

(Paul still sat looking down at her. Suddenly a terrible yell from the wings spun Eudora around in her chair. And then a shrill woman's voice screamed.)

VOICE OFF STAGE: They're diggin'—in the rubbish pit. There's something sticking out! A hand! . . . Somebody's hand!

(Paul jumped lightly down from the table, his back to the audience, his back to her, and the knife clutched in his right hand. He looked down at the knife. He closed it carefully and put it in his pocket.)

Paul whirled around, smiled down at her, and called out to the audience, "That does it!" He looked back at Eudora. With a great effort she got up, aware of applause from beyond the lights. She walked woodenly down the steps ahead of Paul and heard Romaine's voice call, "Paul. Had I been you I would have carved my initials in the table with the knife. I should have done it rather as though the table were a throat."

When Paul sat down, Eudora sank into the seat beside him. The students who were to do the next scene were removing the table and chairs from the stage. She looked at Paul. Then she saw the small 5 x 7" notebook on the seat just beyond him. She reached across and picked it up. His initials in gold were in one corner. She opened it. The paper inside was unruled. She turned her head and saw him watching her, with quiet surprise on his face. She opened the book, riffled through the few scrawled notes. She stopped at a blank sheet of paper with the bottom half torn off.

"Want to borrow some paper?" he asked.

For an answer she tore out the already torn sheet. She went back to her own seat and matched it to the piece in her purse which Draska had given her. The two pieces fitted perfectly.

Chapter Seventeen: WOMAN IN THIS HUMOR

PROFESSOR BREWER shepherded the five of them into the empty classroom next to his office. There he explained that he would give them three tests, allowing 20 minutes for each. As he distributed mimeographed sheets, Eudora looked around at the other four guinea pigs. There was nothing unusual in seeing a few students crouched over the wide arms of lecture chairs in a classroom into which late sunlight fell. She had been one of many such groups during her three years at college. What made today's group seem unusual was that she knew quite well the point of this meeting. Either at Tuck's instigation, or on his own hook, Brewer intended to find out whether one of them happened to be mad.

She looked at the faces about her. Meg was a little amused. Oliver Clarey's black brows were drawn together in a frown of anticipatory concentration. Draska was being elaborately bored. Paul Ober had a calm, quiet look. She suddenly wondered what expression her own face wore.

Brewer laid several stapled sheets face down on the arm of her chair, looked at his watch and said, "Begin."

Eudora turned the paper face up and saw that it was the standard IQ test, which they had all taken in the required psychology course, and which Brewer was giving them again in order to learn whether any mental deterioration had taken place since their Freshman year.

Next was the Humm-Walsworth Temperament Scale, and the last test had been designed, she could see, to reveal the student's ethical orientation. She stated firmly that if she needed a job to meet a pressing financial obligation, she still would not lie about her age, even though by adding one year she would almost certainly get the job. She paused to wonder whether that was after all the ethical reaction. Perhaps it would show a finer spirit to lie and pay the debt. Time pushed her on to the next question.

At the end of the hour Professor Brewer collected the last test papers, thanked them and said, "I should like to question each of you a little further, and along more personal lines. My chapel hours and noon hours are free, as yours are. I have prepared a chart which I will pass among you. Please write your name under the day and hour which will be most convenient."

Eudora signed in the last space—noon hour, Friday—

saw Paul Ober going out the door and followed him.

They walked in silence down the stairs and along the lower hall. "Let's get a coke," suggested Eudora.

"Fine."

When they had gone halfway down the walk to the steps of Old College, Eudora could contain herself no longer. She looked at Paul and realized how inscrutable a profile can be. "Paul, why did you vote against ringing up the curtain Friday?"

His steps slowed just a trifle. "Call it a gesture."

"Were you that fond of Ann?"

"She was a swell girl." He looked fleetingly at Eudora.

"Then it was a matter of delicacy? You felt it was callous to continue the show when she was lying dead?"

"I didn't think of it that way. It just seemed to me that someone should remember her a little."

"That's unusual, and rather sweet."

The words goaded him, as she hoped they would. "Sweet nothing. It just didn't matter to me whether we went on with the show or not. So I voted the way I felt." He looked candidly at her. "I've enlisted in the Air Corps. I have about a thousand hours."

"Paul! What a surprise!"

He looked at her again. "I'm tired of this dream stuff."

Eudora slumped low in the wicker rocker, smoking a before-dinner cigarette. She talked to herself.

Was I really frightened by Paul playing a paranoic? Or did I subconsciously want to be frightened, in order that I might believe he's mad, and therefore that he killed Ann? All my thinking is apparently determined by a desire to escape from the thought that Ames is a killer. And so I see ghosts and dream up fanciful theories. Paul says he's joining the Air Force. What do I do? I think of it as an attempt at flight from an environment which his foul deeds have dirtied for him.

She found that she had been watching two flies on the window pane. They zigzagged up the glass in a futile desperate way, and one took flight. The other followed, and she watched them circle on air in a witless frenzy, dart suddenly together, and part again, one escaping, one pursuing.

Flies have it easy, she thought. *So do all the lower animals. No clash of minds, no fearful doubts. A simple mating, after a while eggs, and nature's plan is served. Why should the very factor of intelligence, which sets the human race apart, so often step in to butch up the animal level, on which the race must exist with a certain degree of happiness if it is to continue? Maybe it's going to be the dinosaurs all over again. They went because they were too big and too dumb to adapt themselves to a changed environment. Maybe we'll go too, because we're too smart. We'll become at last lost in a world of abstractions and principles, and stop having babies.*

York on the falling birth rate, she thought dryly.

The buzzer sounded three times which meant she was wanted down at the desk. When she got there she saw a large oblong package wrapped in brown paper. "It's all yours," the girl on duty told her. "It came by special messenger, just now."

Eudora's heart gave a dull thud as she picked it up. It was addressed in Ames's large and dashing hand. She trudged upstairs with it, set it on her desk, and with a pair of scissors from Millicent's sewing basket cut the thick twine that bound it. Tearing away the heavy wrapping paper, she saw that the box inside was of corrugated board and felt oddly chill to the touch.

Then the door opened, and Millicent came in. Three girls passing in the hall outside on their way downstairs saw the box and stood in the doorway watching.

"Eudora's got a box"—"Open it up!"—"From home?"

Millicent set her books down on her bed and stood at

Eudora's elbow. "Who is it from, Eudora?"

"Ames." Eudora pried the lid up and saw that the box was insulated with dry ice. A smaller box was inside. She opened the end, lifted it out and shook. A frozen fish glided stiffly onto the green blotter.

"A fish! How marvelous!"

"You'll have to have it stuffed and mounted, Eudora!"

"What *are* you going to do with it?"

"Sleep with it under my pillow, naturally," said Eudora.

"Look." Millicent pointed. "There's a card inside the box." The card said, *Sweets to the sweet.*

Downstairs in the lounge someone began to play the piano: *Liebestraum.*

"My dream of love, I dream of you and roses telling of love so true," sang one of the girls in the doorway. Then the dinner bell rang, and they went away laughing.

"Well!" said Millicent.

Eudora looked up from the card. "He's trying to show me that he's regained his sense of humor," she said, and realized too late that Millicent wouldn't understand.

He's calling me a frozen fish, she told herself. She picked up the fish to take it down to the kitchen. *He did go fishing, then. But how long does it take to catch a fish?*

Then a thought slid obliquely into her mind: *Sweets to the sweet.* And the fish was dead.

Before going into the dining hall she stopped at the mailboxes. There was one letter for her—a long white envelope containing an elaborately worded summons to the coroner's inquest on the death of Ann Laird, to be held on Saturday morning at nine o'clock.

Tuck sat hunched at his desk making a schedule of Ann Laird's last hour on earth:

11:00 The final curtain. Ann got the key to the prop room from Joe, and then listened to Romaine.

11:30 Had finished removing costume and make-up,

and had already left the girls' dressing-room, presumably
for the prop room.

11:40 Draska knocked at dressing-room door to tell
women to hurry. Meg entered dressing-room to see if anyone was ready to go to Carlo's, and Nora sent her after
Ann. She looked into the theater, didn't see Ann, went to
prop room.

11:50 Meg saw light in prop room go out.

12:00 Oliver phoned Ann's home; she had not returned.

Ann, then, had gone out the front door of Old College,
down the steps and around the building to the prop
room before Ober, Clarey and Meg Fife stood there talking and smoking. The murderer could also have gone to
the prop room before about 11:35. He did not leave before 11:50, when Meg saw the light in the prop room go
out. At that time Ober and Clarey both said they were sitting a block away in Oliver's car. They, then, did not kill
Ann Laird, unless Meg had been mistaken about seeing
the light go out at 11:50. Or was lying about it. Why
would she lie about it? One obvious reason was that if she
herself had killed Ann before she stood smoking and talking with Ober and Clarey, the lie about the light would
be a shrewd means of casting suspicion elsewhere. If she
had been mistaken about the light—if she had been the
innocent victim of an optical illusion, either Clarey or
Ober could have killed Ann before having a cigarette on
the porch.

But if Meg really did see the light go out, the murderer
was standing in the prop room at 11:45, and was someone
other than Meg, Oliver, or Paul Ober.

As a matter of cold fact, anyone in the building could
have committed the murder and gone merrily on to
Carlo's afterward. *I think*, he decided, *that I'll let the matter of opportunity rest. All of them had the opportunity
to kill her, that's plain. What I need to know is which of
them had a motive. And what the motive was. And until I*

hear from Brewer, my hands are tied.

In the next three days—Wednesday, Thursday, and Friday—Tuck kept rather busy.

Eudora kept busy, too. She typed and handed in the paper which was due, and did some studying for final examinations. This took a great deal of will power. At noon on Friday she appeared in Professor Brewer's office to be questioned. As soon as she entered, he stood up.

"I'd like to take an electro-encephalogram first," he told her. "We'll have to go down to the psychology laboratories in the basement."

They entered the section of the basement devoted to the psychology laboratories by a front door to the left of the steps, and concealed by shrubbery. The laboratories were a confusing clutter of equipment, and as the bottoms of the windows were on a level with the green lawn in front of Old College, Eudora never entered them without being immediately conscious of a buried feeling.

Brewer stopped at an armchair completely surrounded by copper mesh to exclude interference from any extraneous ether waves. He motioned for Eudora to seat herself; she did so with the same sense of indignity she had once felt on a doctor's examination table.

So she chatted. "I didn't know that encephalograms were very reliable."

Professor Brewer attached an electrode to the left side of her head and said, "Oh, they'll reveal any decided deviation from normal."

"I'm willing to take an oath that I haven't got epilepsy or a brain tumor."

"How nice for you," grinned Brewer.

"Is it true that a student tried to take one of these last semester and got Beethoven's *Fifth?*"

"Yes. He forgot to close the victim completely in, and picked up the broadcast of a local radio station. Don't talk for a few minutes, please."

So Eudora folded her hands in her lap while the pattern made by her waking brain was plucked out of her skull by means of the electrodes, which transmitted the energy to a fine copper wire, which intercepted a beam of light falling on a slowly turning roll of sensitized paper in a camera. She thought, *Wouldn't it be funny if I do have a brain tumor, or am epileptic?* ...

When Brewer finally removed the electrodes he said, "Now you can talk again."

"This may surprise you," confided Eudora, "but I have been known to be completely silent for as long as an hour at a stretch."

"It does," said Brewer.

They went out the front door then and up the steps of Old College. In Brewer's second-floor office he seated her in a lecture chair, facing the light, and sat down at his desk. "Now for a few questions," he said. "You are how old?"

"Twenty-two."

"Any brothers or sisters?"

"No."

"Your parents are alive?"

"Yes."

"And what is your father's occupation?"

Squashing a desire to say, *He's a trap drummer of no mean ability*, she said, "Doctor."

"You live with them?"

"No. I live at the girls' dorm. My parents are in San Francisco."

"Can you think of any recent dream you have had?"

The dream of escaping through a forest in a white gown was as vivid in her mind as it had been when she awoke from its spell, but she said, "No." It sounded a little defiant.

"Whom do you like best, your father or your mother?"

"My father, I think. That is, I admire him for what

he does."

"Do you have a sweetheart?"

"Just at present, no."

"Changing partners, hm? But you have recently 'dated' with one special young man?"

"Yes."

"What were your feelings toward him?"

"Mixed. He was a very attractive chap, but I didn't respect him."

"Oh? May I ask why?"

Eudora wanted to say, *No, you may not,* but said instead, "Let's say it was a matter of different early environments. I have been brought up in the belief that people are important for what they do, not for how they look, or how much money they happen to have."

"This chap of whom you speak was more or less of a ne'er-do-well?"

"That's putting it rather harshly. Let's say that he has never had the opportunity to learn that life is anything but a delightful game."

"I take it, then, that you broke off the friendship."

"That's right."

To her relief he took another tack. "Do you have any close woman friend?"

"Just now, my closest friend is my roommate, Millicent Legg."

"What are your feelings toward her?"

"Well, she irritates me sometimes, but on the whole I'm quite fond of her. I'm a little sorry for her, too. She's struggling through the last stages of adolescence and is hampered by a terrific silver brace, complete with twanging rubber bands."

"But you have no deep aversion to her? Nothing like the lack of admiration you felt for this young man?"

"Oh, no. She's an extremely studious girl, with a highly intelligent mind. I rather admire her earnestness."

"Have you ever had a severe illness?"

"Tonsillitis, at the age of twelve."

"Do you have at present any financial anxieties?"

"No."

"Have you any regrets about the stand you took toward that young man?"

"No."

Then came the bomb. Brewer leaned forward, and those vitreous eyes of his looked very kindly into hers. "Would you like to tell me what's worrying you? I may be able to help."

She found herself sitting very straight. "Nothing's worrying me."

"Sometimes," persisted Brewer, "when we are young, we are apt to let what we think life *should* be get in the way of our evaluation of life as it *is*." He leaned far back in his chair. One arm was stretched out over the surface of the desk while the fingers of that hand toyed with the exceedingly sharp point of a pencil. "Are you sure you wouldn't like to tell me what's the matter?"

"Nothing's the matter," repeated Eudora, doggedly.

The coroner was a fussy little man, with exactly six strands of hair combed with care over his bald dome. The coroner's jury looked as though it had been picked at random from passers-by in the street. The inquest was held in a small courtroom. The coroners sat at a raised desk; a court reporter sat below it. Jim Laird identified the body; the doctor testified she had died from a blow on the head; Eudora told of finding the body; Brewer also told of finding the body; Tuck summed up the findings of the police, which were not impressive. The jury of eight slowly declined from mild interest to a boredom painful to watch. At long last, the coroner passed the palm of his hand over his dome and reached across his desk for the written findings of the jury, handed up to him by the usher. Only his eyes moved as he scanned the square white paper. Then he let a glance of vague malevolence rove the room. No one was at all surprised when he read portentously, "As a result of this inquest into the death of Mrs. Ann Laird, we find that she died at approximately midnight, on June 9, 1940, in the 'properties room' in Old College of Southwest University, by a blow on the head, at the hands of a person or persons unknown."

As he walked down the long marble corridor of the Hall of Justice, someone fell into step beside him, and Tuck looked down into Eudora York's face.

"Why do they bother having these things?" she asked. "Do they ever establish anything definite?"

"As a rule," said Tuck, "they do. The verdict you heard today is rather the exception. Usually, you see, the police know who did it by the time the inquest is held."

"You look glum," she said.

"And you look very cheerful," he replied.

After leaving Eudora, Tuck went into a drugstore and telephoned the university, asking for Professor Brewer's office. "This is Tuck," he said. "Have you found anything?"

"Yes. They're all sane."

"All sane?"

"The Clarey boy shows the widest divergence from normal. His intelligence is average, but he's low on stability and he has practically no sense of ethics. Paul Ober has a slightly lower IQ than Clarey, but a high degree of emotional stability; his sense of ethics is good. The Fife girl came out a few points this side of genius, a high degree of stability and a high ethical sense. Draska also has a high IQ, is also stable and has normal ethical perceptions. York interested me the most. Her grade on the IQ test went down nine points from what it was two and a half years ago. Nor did she do as well as I believe her capable of on the other two tests. Something is worrying her, Tuck, more than perhaps she knows. I make that statement not only on the basis of these tests, but also on my observation of her in class for the past week. She is an exceedingly alert student, and in the past we have had several whopping good arguments. But during the last two lectures she's paid very little attention. Her replies to the questions on the temperament test were not consistent. I would be inclined to consider her a case of low emotional stability, had I not seen her, you will remember, face to face with a dead body. Her reaction at that time indicated an unusually high degree of control, even allowing for the fact that she and Ann Laird were acquaintances rather than friends. Altogether, the whole picture adds up in my mind to the fact that her attention is being sapped by some gnawing personal worry. When I questioned her at noon yesterday, I learned that she has no financial problems. I asked her bluntly what was worrying her, and she got her back up. I am fairly certain that whatever is bothering her has to do with a young man from whom she had recently parted. I don't know who he is. But in your place, I should certainly look into it. It may be simply difference in temperament, but what she told me about him makes me want to know more. I doubt if you can learn anything from her, but her roommate might be helpful. The roommate's name is Millicent Legg, and she'll have to be handled carefully because they are rather good friends."

"Thanks," said Tuck.

"Not at all."

Tuck then telephoned the dormitory and invited Millicent Legg to lunch.

Chapter Eighteen: WITHOUT EMOTION

`MISS LEGG,` asked Tuck, when Millicent was busy with a shrimp cocktail, "does Miss York have a boy friend?"

"Well," reflected Millicent. "More or less."

"What do you mean by that?"

Millicent wiped the corners of her mouth daintily and reached for water; her hand was tiny around the thick bulge of the glass. "There's a boy who is very fond of her, and she's fond of him, but they don't get along."

"Why not?"

"He's crazy," said Millicent.

"Crazy!"

"Oh, I don't mean really crazy. I was using the word in its colloquial sense."

"I see. You mean he's a bit wacky?"

"I mean that he's unstable."

"I see."

"He does things like sending her a fish."

"A goldfish, you mean?"

"No. A dead, frozen fish. I guess he caught it, but it's still not a sensible thing to do."

"What other nonsensical things does he do?"

"The week after they met he sent her a record player and six symphony albums. She'd mentioned that she was fond of music."

"He sounds nice—to me."

"But don't you see, Eudora couldn't accept such an expensive gift from a man she'd just met. She sent 'em back. He never did seem to get the point."

"How long have they known each other?"

"They met at a dance his fraternity gave last semester. He danced with her almost all evening." Millicent sounded just a trifle wistful.

"What do you think of him?"

"I've only seen him half a dozen times, but I think he's fine, only not for Eudora." She paused. "You see, in the first place, he's very rich. And that's a disadvantage, because his sense of values is automatically different from hers. He doesn't have any social consciousness." She paused again. "And also he makes a mistake in letting her know he likes her a lot."

"Is that bad?"

"It's bad with a person like Eudora. She would deeply appreciate a boy who was wrapped up in medicine, or law, and let her know it. Once when he was waiting downstairs for Eudora and I happened to pass by, I got talking with him, and I told him that. And he said, 'She'll have to take me as I am. I won't pretend.' "

"Rather an egotist, wouldn't you say?"

"I would. But not an egotism coming from an over-valuation of himself. I think it's more like an egotism coming from an unusual freedom from misfortune."

"What's his name?"

"Ames. Ames Hanna."

"You said she was fond of him. Present tense?"

"Oh, yes."

"Has she seen him lately?"

"Yes. She saw him on the night Ann died. I was eating dinner in the Wagon Wheel, alone. I looked out the window and saw a car parked in front of Old College. I thought, 'My, but that looks like Ames's car.' You see, it's rather a terrific thing, black and shining and half a block long. And then I saw them, on the porch of Old College. He seemed to be holding her wrists, and it looked as though they might be arguing. Then the waitress came with my order, and someone spoke to me, and when I looked back, they were walking together out to his car. They drove away."

"Do you think anything could have happened that night that made her worried about him?"

Millicent's eyes opened wide. "It's funny, but I've wondered that myself. Eudora's been strange lately. And when he sent her that dead fish Tuesday night, I caught a very funny look on her face. She looked frightened, Mr. Tuck."

"She didn't happen to discuss the reason for her odd

behavior?"

"No. And I didn't ask her. You don't do that with
Eudora. She didn't say anything about having seen Ames,
and I didn't tell her I'd seen her go off with him. It
wouldn't have been delicate, because she'd refused to have
dinner with me, you see."

"Oh. You mean that she must have planned to eat with
him instead of with you?"

Millicent shook her head slowly. "I don't think so. I
think he took her more or less by surprise. She wasn't
really dressed to go out dining--she just had on a very
plain white school dress; and no hat."

"A white dress, did you say?" asked Tuck.

"Yes," said Millicent.

The Hannas' house was in a canyon in Bel-Air--a canyon quite consciously a haven apart from the sunny stucco
of sprawling, middle-class Los Angeles. Great houses, in
every style of architecture, stood well back from the
twisting road on the canyon's floor, and were half-hidden
by old live oaks that cast their shadows on façades that
faced the west. There was a great quiet; without the
houses the canyon would have been a melancholy place
—even their presence did not quite destroy that sense of
aboriginal solitude. Driving past the opulence of a Geor-
gian house, Tuck smiled to see it hemmed in on all sides
by the brown and furtive wildness of trees and fallen
leaves and underbrush. The greens here were somber; the
sunlight even this early in the afternoon did not touch
the careful lawns and low, pruned shrubs, under the
old trees that had been here long before the houses came.

The Hanna house was rambling and Spanish, and the
warm gold of its walls looked friendly. He drove his pro-
saic sedan across a small bridge that spanned a trickle
of brown water and parked under a dying oak tree over-
hanging a cobbled area designed to hold a number of

larger cars than his. He walked up wide and shallow steps of dull turquoise tiles and thudded an old wrought-iron knocker against a scarlet door, which was opened by a trim, middle-aged housekeeper. He heard music.

"I'd like to speak to Ames Hanna," said Tuck. "I telephoned ahead; he expects me."

"Please come in," she said, and led him to a large room, high-ceilinged and white-walled, full of calm and rich color which did not offset a general atmosphere of coolness intruding from the canyon outside. Ames rose as he entered. He had been sitting in a low armchair beside a tremendous radio, listening to Mozart.

"I haven't the slightest idea why you want to see me," Ames said, as he extended his hand. "What have I done? And please sit down."

The soft harmonies crossed the quiet air to their ears. "Perhaps I should turn that off," said Ames. Tuck watched him move to the radio with a springy grace as youthful as his expression. As Tuck sat down in an armchair deep and soft and somewhat enervating, Ames returned from the silenced radio and slouched in a similar chair, separated from Tuck's by a small table. "Would you like a drink?" Ames seemed genuinely at a loss and making the best of it.

"Thanks, no. I'll tell you why I'm here. I have just learned you were at Southwest University last Thursday night."

Ames looked puzzled. "Yes, I was."

"I thought you might possibly know something that will help me."

"Help you? In what way?"

"Perhaps I should have explained that I'm investigating the murder."

Ames sat slowly up. "What murder?"

"You don't know that a girl was killed there last Thursday night?"

Ames shook his head decidedly. "This is the first I've

heard of it."

"You've been away from town?"

"I left on a fishing trip Thursday night, and I didn't get back until Tuesday afternoon. I never read the papers anyway. Who was murdered?"

"A woman named Ann Laird. She was hit on the head in the properties room at Old College."

"Good Lord!"

"Knowing that you were at the building on that evening, I was in hopes you might have seen something."

"When was she killed?"

"About midnight."

"Oh. Well, I was almost to Catalina Island by then. I was only on campus for a half hour, at dinnertime."

"And you didn't return later?"

Ames looked annoyed. "I told you I went fishing. We have a motorboat at the yacht harbor at Wilmington. It's fine, crossing the channel by moonlight. I often do it when I want to get away for a while."

"You were alone?"

"Yes." Ames leaned back in his chair again. "Why do you think I should know something about this murder, Mr. Tuck? I don't know the girl who was killed. Did someone tell you I did?"

"No."

"And who told you I was on campus that night?"

Tuck grinned at him. "I'm asking the questions."

A sullen look came over Ames Hanna's face, to be replaced at once by a lopsided smile. "If you aren't going to have a drink, I am. Excuse me."

While he was gone, Tuck looked about the room. He wondered why he was deeply disturbed by the fact that this Ames had a ready explanation that exactly covered the crucial period of time during which one woman had been killed and two attacked.

Ames came back with a tall tinkling glass and again

slumped deep in the armchair beside Tuck's.

"Why did you send Eudora York a dead fish?" Tuck asked, abruptly.

There was a short, tense silence. Ames's voice was bleak when he spoke. "It was just a joke."

"It was a queer joke."

"I'm a queer guy."

"One more question. Do you recall what color dress Eudora York had on when you took her to dinner Thursday night?"

"White. I noticed it particularly because white isn't becoming to her."

"Do you know that she was frightened by that fish you sent to her?"

"Frightened!" Ames shook his head slowly from side to side. "I don't get it."

"What are your feelings toward Miss York, Ames?"

"They are my own affair," said Ames evenly.

"And hers toward you?"

He smiled without mirth. "You've got me. But from what you've said, I gather that for some reason she thinks I'm mixed up in the murder of a woman I never saw in my life. Isn't that right, Tuck?"

"Are you sure you've never seen her? Perhaps this will refresh your memory." From his pocket Tuck drew one of the photographs taken by the police of Ann Laird lying dead. It was glossy and ghastly-clear and had been taken from a point directly above her body.

Ames looked down at the dead face, which seemed to be looking straight into the camera, backed by the black bloodstain. His only reaction was very faint disgust.

"I've never seen her," he repeated, handing the picture back to Tuck. "She's young, isn't she?"

"Only a year older than Miss York."

"Do you have any idea who killed her?"

"Oh, I have ideas," said Tuck. "Ideas are cheap. **What**

I need is a motive."

Ames tilted his glass, lowered it and rubbed his nose childishly where the ice had bumped it. Tuck stood up.

"Going?" asked Ames.

"Yes."

Ames rose and walked with him to the front door. "Sorry I couldn't help."

Tuck looked swiftly at him. The face was devoid of expression, but a certain malice, like the malice of a naughty little boy, was sparkling in the narrow hazel eyes.

Beating a retreat down the silent canyon, Tuck looked about him. The sun had lowered, and the houses facing west no longer wore their smiling sunlight. Dusk was beginning to gather here, and night would come sooner to the dwellers in this crevasse in the hills than to the simple denizens of the wide city outside its walls. A peculiar affinity between Ames Hanna and the place he lived suggested itself to Tuck. Ames, with his Mozart and his fine tweed coat, was the houses Tuck was passing; something else in Ames corresponded to the native wildness which surrounded them, unaltered and perhaps unalterable.

Chapter Nineteen: THE RIDDLE OF ERRORS

IN THE LEFT wing Eudora presided over a scarred table on whose surface the hand props were ranged. She handed the last of Draska's mother's goblets to a nervous boy in a ruff.

"I don't see why you're twitching," she whispered. "All you have to do is stroll across stage waving your glass to help provide a gala atmosphere."

The boy grinned palely and ran a finger between his neck and the ruff. The boy who was working the curtains peered into the wings to see that the actors were ready, nodded at them, and pulled steadily at the cord which

opened the curtains on the fifth scene of the first act: *A
hall in Capulet's house.*

Eudora coughed. Dave, who had no change of costume
and so watched the entire show from the wings, his mouth
shaping the actor's words, turned on her.

"Will you take that hack out of here?" he whispered.
"That's the third time this evening. If you cough on a big
scene, it's gone." He clamped a thin hand onto Joe's shoulder. "Can you get someone else who knows who gets which
prop?"

"I'll do it," said Joe. "But listen, Eudora. You be back
after the show, see? We're going to strike the set."

"Right," said Eudora, coughed again, saw both of
Dave's hands tremble at his temples, and tiptoed around
behind the rear curtain to the door in the opposite wing.
The balcony, which was a tall wooden table, erratically
braced and topped by a jutting platform surrounded by a
wrought-iron railing, impeded her progress. It almost
filled the space between the rear curtain and the back
wall, the forward side of the railing actually touching the
curtain. For the balcony scene it would be moved forward
so that the platform projected through the parted curtains, the lower structure made invisible by a covering of
dark blue velvet like the rear drop. Since specific staging
was being used throughout the play, the dewberry spot
would center on the balcony to mask its crudity

She measured the distance between the lower structure
and the curtain and decided not to risk it. Nothing was
more disastrous to a scene than the moving bulge of someone fumbling his way behind a curtain. She crawled
carefully through the struts and braces of rough wood,
tore her dress on a nail, cursed softly, and left by the rear
corridor of Old College, while Romeo, his voice loud at
such close range, proclaimed, "What lady's that which
doth enrich the hand of yonder knight?"

There was a moon, and it was a warm night. She looked

up at the moon, round above the dark square mass of the library, and saw it in two ways at the same time. She saw it as a cold small planet, circling around a larger one, on which it cast its borrowed light; she saw it also as the mysterious disk of all poets and lovers.

I wonder which moon is the true moon, she wondered dreamily. *The scientists can prove their cold planet, but long before that, millions had learned that it is the lamp of lovers, a conspirator and an illusion-maker. Gad, girl, you're getting sloppy in your old age,* she told herself.

"Archeozoic, Proterozoic, Mesozoic, Cenozoic, Paleozoic," said Millicent to the ceiling as Eudora opened the door of their room. She was sitting at her desk; her hair was rumpled, and her eyes were wild.

"Same to you, dear," said Eudora.

Millicent removed her eyes from the ceiling. "Geologic periods," she explained. "That's the only final I'm scared of." She bent over the thick book.

Eudora felt a kindliness which all Millicent's tears over Ann's death had not aroused, for Millicent had been almost grotesque in grief, and had displayed a want of restraint which Eudora, on principle, disliked. But now, unaware of anything except the geologic periods, she stood for all the people who had lost something they loved, wept for it, and gone on living as they had lived before.

Eudora lay on her stomach on her bed and opened her copy of Freud's *General Introduction to Psychoanalysis.* She began to review his chapters on errors, but the moon intruded itself. *Now this is really a little silly,* she thought. *Here we sit, on a lovely summer night, memorizing the names of the geological eras and reading Freud.* She suddenly found herself wishing that Ames would call. On a night like this she could ask him some blunt questions, banish the banshee from her mind and laugh with him.

"Never the time, the place, and the loved one all together," she quoted aloud, and then coughed.

Millicent turned vague eyes on her. "Have you done anything for that cough?"

"Millicent, have you ever had a boy friend?"

Millicent shook her head cautiously. "Not exactly. Although the son of one of mother's friends took me to the Hollywood Bowl three times last summer. Music was his hobby. He played the bagpipes."

"Good Lord!"

Millicent said with an undeceptive sprightliness, "It's these braces, you know."

"It's your hair, too," said Eudora, her eyes going critically over Millicent's non-assets. "And that blasted intellect of yours. If you could just pretend you know less than you do, you might snag a man. You want a man, you know."

"Well," said Millicent brightly, "a man doesn't seem to want me, you see."

"Have a cigarette," Eudora suggested, and tossed her the pack from her own bedside table. Millicent caught it with a little bounce, caught a packet of matches, and lighted a cigarette with that effort at extreme casualness common to non-smokers.

Eudora flopped onto her back, propped herself against two pillows and blew smoke at the ceiling. "I'm always amused by these women's-magazine stories where the gal loses ten pounds, changes her hair-do, buys a new outfit and wins back the wandering male. But I can't help believing that a good appearance does a great deal for the ego. If you'll pardon my frankness, Millie, you usually look as though you'd combed your hair with your toothbrush and bought your dress for its durability."

Millicent flushed, but said steadily, "I don't mind your frankness at all. And I wish you'd tell me something else." She leaned forward over the open book. "Do you think I'm psychologically maladjusted to life?"

"Do you?"

Millicent stared painfully at Eudora. "I had a lonely childhood. I never played with other children. I never wanted to. I always enjoyed older people. Children can be so cruel."

"In another day," said Eudora, "you might have something to worry about. Today, we know the damage a childhood lack of adjustment can do, and we know that damage can be remedied by psychoanalysis: by giving the patient full insight into the real cause of his unhappiness. You already seem to have that, so you don't need a psychiatrist. But a good permanent wave might help. And how much longer do you have to wear those braces?"

"My dentist said something about letting me take them off and wear retainers pretty soon."

"Do it right away. Not wearing them would do more good for your ego than wearing them could possibly do for your teeth. And, Millicent, will you hate me if I say that you don't use make-up right? One of the problems of being a woman is that you're expected to do the best you can with whatever you have. It's darned quixotic to overlook that fact. I'm not quixotic. I can put on my face in four minutes by the clock. I do it for the same reason I wear a skirt. It has to be done."

Millicent was silent for a moment. Then she said, "Eudora, would you fix me up? Tonight? To show me?"

"Sure. I'll do it right now." Eudora went to her dresser and returned with the businesslike tin box in which she kept her cosmetics. "Bring over that low chair," she said. "No, wait. First wash your face."

In a few minutes Millicent was sitting below Eudora, who was perched on the edge of her bed, and her face was tilted back in the light of Eudora's reading lamp. Eudora worked swiftly for ten minutes. Then she leaned back to survey her work and was pleased. "There. Go look," she said, and began putting away the lipstick, the rouge, the powder base, the eye shadow.

Millicent went to the mirror of her dresser, her back to Eudora. She stood for a long moment looking at her reflection. It was not a transformation, Eudora knew, but Millicent's eyes protruded less because of brown eye shadow, her mouth was almost pretty and her skin was clear and smooth. She saw Millicent put up one wondering hand and touch her cheek. Then she said, "Thank you, Eudora." She turned back to her reflection, and Eudora was amused to see her tilt her head to one side in unconscious coquetry.

So what happened an hour later surprised Eudora considerably.

Eudora, her mind at last glued to Freud on errors, coughed. Millicent got up from her desk and went over to the medicine chest above the washbasin. "I saved about two doses of that cough medicine the doctor gave me for my throat last winter."

"Don't want any."

Millicent went right on looking. "It's not gooey, darling. It goes down like water. Let's see—I put it into a small empty bottle I had. Mercurochrome. aspirin, nose drops. . . "

Eudora glanced up impatiently from her book. "I don't want any," she repeated.

Millicent, on tiptoe to reach the top shelf, looked at Eudora over her shoulder. "You're going to get a large spoonful," she stated.

Eudora smiled to herself. Her theory, that Millicent's interior would benefit by a slight alteration of Millicent's exterior, seemed already to be bearing fruit. A latent assurance was emerging.

"All right, darling," she said. "Don't browbeat."

She became aware that Millicent was standing beside the bed. She laid her book on her lap and watched her carefully pour a brown liquid into a large spoon from a very small bottle. Eudora opened her mouth. The spoon approached steadily, and just as she felt it click coldly against her lower teeth, her eye fell on the bottle in Millicent's other hand. The label bore a red skull and crossbones and the word POISON!

She jerked her head back and yelled, "Hey!"

Millicent's baffled eyes went to the bottle at which Eudora was still staring. She gave a shrill little laugh. "I got the iodine by mistake. How terrible. The bottles are *exactly* the same size. I'd poured what was left of the cough stuff into a small bottle because the cabinet was so crowded. . . . Oh, Eudora, if you'd swallowed it!"

She went to the medicine cabinet again, and Eudora leaned slowly back against the pillows. The paragraph she had just been reading galloped across her mind in jerky phrases—"*Errors . . . not accidents; serious mental acts . . . they arise through the mutual interference of two different intentions . . .*"

Two different intentions. Now why, she wondered, *does Millicent have a subconscious desire to poison me?*

When Eudora reached Touchstone Theater the curtains were open and on the brightly lighted stage Joe and Draska and several members of the properties staff were arguing about what to do with the balcony.

"Why tear it apart?" Joe was saying. "It took time and trouble to build. Maybe we'll need a tall riser for a show sometime."

"The railing has to go back tomorrow," said a prop man. "I didn't buy it from that junk dealer, he just rented it to us."

"Where's Juliet's dagger?" called a woman's voice from the wings.

"Say," said Draska to Joe. "I just remembered. My mother needs those goblets of hers for a dinner tomorrow."

"I'm glad to see *you*," said the girl in the wings who was laying small props in a large clothes basket. "I don't know which of these belong to us and which belong to kind friends and relations."

"I have the list," Eudora said. "You go home."

While the argument over the balcony proceeded, one of the men took advantage of Joe and Dave's absorption to slip quietly away, and Eudora laid props to rest in the basket or lined them up on the table so that their owners could claim them later. Mrs. Draska's goblets, which were very fine indeed, she began to pack again in the box in which Draska had brought them.

"I say let it wait till morning," she heard Draska say. "I'm dead."

"So am I," said Joe, grimly.

Eudora, wondering, *Why is it that when you try to pack something in its original container, the container always seems to have shrunk*, heard Draska call, "Put out the lights when you leave, Eudora." Footsteps echoed up the aisle of the empty theater.

I'll finish this and go, she decided. When the last goblet was in place, she remembered about Juliet's missing dagger. It was a Moorish dagger, purchased in Spain by Miss Fitch in days gone by, and was dear to her heart.

Meg probably left it on stage, she decided, and crossed the boards that looked so stark under the lights. It was not lying where she had fallen, stage center. She stood there, one hand over her eyes, wondering, *Now what would I have done with the dagger if I had been Meg?*

It was not a sound that made her turn. It was a feeling that something was happening behind her. What she saw froze her where she stood for a moment. The balcony, with its formidable iron railing, was tilting slowly forward, straight toward her.

She jumped. She twisted her ankle and fell. The balcony crashed to the floor exactly where she had been standing. Louder than the splintering crackle of wood was the metallic thump of the railing hitting the stage.

She turned her head toward the rear of the stage and saw Ames standing there, backed by the dark curtains, his face strange.

Like a statue blessed suddenly with the power of motion, Ames came swiftly toward where she sat, saying, "Eudora! Oh, Eudora! Are you all right?" He grasped her limp hands and swung her to her feet.

"What are you doing here?" she asked.

"Waiting for you. Millicent played Cupid and told me that if I hung around until after the show I might get a chance to see you alone."

Eudora's eyes went to the sprawling balcony.

"As I stepped forward to grab you before you followed the rest of them out, my coat caught on a nail sticking out from that—that monstrosity." He twisted and looked ruefully down at a ragged rip in his sleeve.

Eudora looked at him. It seemed that she would never be able to unfasten her eyes from his candid face. "Why were you behind the curtain?"

"Why not? It seemed as good a place as any to lurk." As he said the words, he looked straight at her. Then a look of unbelief came over his face. "What are you thinking?" he asked very softly.

She said nothing.

He took a step closer to her. "And why did you send the detective to question me?"

"Don't come any closer!" Eudora whispered.

The look of unbelief on his face intensified. With no word, he turned his back and left her standing there.

When Eudora reached the dormitory, she did not go to her room. She went to the telephone, once more looked up Professor Brewer's number, and dialed it. After several rings he answered, sounding cross.

"This is Eudora York, Professor Brewer. There's something I must know. Are they all sane?"

"Are all who sane—oh. You saw through my little contribution to justice-shall-be-done. Yes, they were all quite sane, including yourself, Miss York."

The receiver made a final sound as she hung it up.

Chapter Twenty: AGAINST WET FEET

TUCK AND Froody were lingering over Sunday-morning breakfast. Sunlight filled Tuck's flat, which was on top of a hill in an old, neglected section of downtown Los Angeles. The flat, which was rented unfurnished, contained solid armchairs, a sturdy sofa and an upright piano. The bed had been built especially for Tuck and was both long and wide. The air now was filled with smoke from Tuck's cigarettes and Froody's cigar, a fat little cigar shaped a little like Froody himself.

"If Brewer is right, and we have no reason to believe that he's not, five of our suspects have been eliminated at one stroke, if the killer is insane. That gives us this: The murder, if committed because of insanity, was committed by the husband, or Professor Romaine, or the girl's best friend, or some anonymous person who knew she was going to the prop room. If the murderer is not insane, the murder was committed by one of these people, plus the five students Brewer examined. Let's take a look at our reasons for believing the killer to be insane. First, the method used—violence. Second, the coffin ad. Third, the phone call to Laird. Fourth, the attack on Miss York. Fifth, the attack on Miss Fife."

"You've forgotten the angle that there's no motive for a sane murder," said Froody.

"I left that out on purpose. Because all we can say is that we don't know of a sane motive. Now, how about the facts supporting a sane murderer. First, the method—

"But you used that to show the murderer is insane!"

"Sure. On the basis of what we know now, it can apply either way. I can think of circumstances that might make a sane man, setting out to murder, use that method. I also know that it's a means of killing frequently used by the insane. So it has to be added in both places. What else? Oh. The cigarette butts. They could mean someone waited there for the girl. And then, the body having been moved after death might mean that the murderer wanted his murder to pass for an accident. He might then have become flustered and turned out the lights, defeating his purpose. In fact, we have some idea of what upset him, because we know that Fife was outside the inner door calling the dead girl's name shortly after the murder must have happened. Can you think of any other reason for believing that our killer is sane?"

"I don't even like those," said Froody.

"And just to complicate the picture, York is apparently alarmed about her boy friend. I talked to him today. He's a pretty smooth number. He was on the campus the night Laird was killed. He says he left on a fishing trip several hours before she died. He was gone until Tuesday. He went alone. I've checked with the clubhouse at the yacht basin where his motorboat is kept. He left, all right, at ten on Thursday night. And he returned on Tuesday afternoon. But that doesn't mean he went to Catalina. And it doesn't mean he went fishing. Maybe he docked somewhere else, and went hunting—with a two-by-four."

"I get it—he knows Laird?"

"He says he never saw her in his life. But Eudora York was wearing a white dress the night Laird was killed. They're the same height and heft, and they both have brown hair."

"You mean he could have gone after his girl, and got Laird by error?"

"That did occur to me."

"He'd have to of come up behind her."

"Well, couldn't he? Think of the setup. The cigarette butts—someone waiting. A figure in white passes him in the darkness, enters the prop room. He whacks her. Then maybe something not quite right hits him. He turns her over. It's a stranger. So he tries again, twice."

"Boy, what a hate!"

"And that bothers me a little. Because my guess is that he loves her. Well, it's a new angle for you to chew on."

"He'd be crazy, of course."

"Oh, of course. But I know that won't worry you."

"Well, old girl," Eudora said to her reflection in the mirror, "if I didn't know you so well, I'd say you had a persecution complex."

She grinned palely. *It's trying to the nerves,* she decided, *to believe that attempts have been made on your life by (a) your roommate and (b) your sweetheart. So I'll put a green ribbon in my hair and go forth into the bright Sabbath morning, pretending nothing is the matter.*

Millicent was sitting alone on the porch. She was dressed in black. "The funeral is at one," she said.

Eudora stopped in her tracks. "Oh. I'd forgotten."

"Eudora!"

"I'll be back in an hour or two," promised Eudora.

When she reached the theater, Joe, Dave Draska and one prop man were standing around the balcony.

"What did you do last night, decide to carry it down by yourself?" asked Joe.

"Obviously," said Eudora. "It was too heavy."

"Then you can give us a hand now," said Joe.

After unscrewing the railing, they managed to manipulate the balcony out of the door in the right wing, along the corridor, and down the rear stair to the basement. Joe dropped the front corner and ran ahead to open the door to the prop room. He came back looking a little odd.

"Her blood's still on the floor," he said.

No one said anything.

It was not until they had worked the balcony through the door and set it up in the corner near the army cot that Eudora saw it.

The right of the two high windows was without its pane of glass. The fragments were lying on the floor beneath it, and through the startlingly empty window frame, Eudora could see the long trunk of a palm tree rising serene to the sky.

Tuck and Froody and the fingerprint man, whose name registered on Eudora's mind as something very like Varnish, stood around her as she pointed down at the pieces of the broken window. Tuck stooped and examined them. He looked up at Froody. "Happened before the rain was over." Eudora looked more closely. A fine film of dust lay over the pieces of glass, spotted in places by round spots with uneven edges.

It hadn't happened last night, then. Ames had entered the building, for whatever reason, through the door. The thought was mildly cheering, but was only a moment's ripple in the pool of quite uncaring calmness which her mind had become. "Après moi, practically anything," she said to herself, and went over to the army cot, where she curled her feet beneath her skirt, leaned against the cold plaster of the wall, and lighted a cigarette, dropping the match into the brass vase which Brewer had utilized as an ash tray the morning this crazy pattern began to weave itself into her days and nights.

She watched for almost an hour. while under the two dangling electric bulbs which seemed to be hanging as low as possible in order to watch. the fingerprint man busied himself with both light and dark powders. and Tuck and Froody slowly circled the room referring with low murmurs to the sheaf of large glossy photographs in Tuck's big hand. Then they faced toward where she sat and looked from a photograph to the six-inch space between the bottom of the Chinese screen and the floor, and back again at their picture. They both squatted solemnly and sighted under the screen.

Tuck came over in two strides and folded the screen together with a clatter. "Nope," he said. "They're gone."

"Yeah," said Froody, walking to Tuck's side and standing on tiptoe to peer at the photograph. "But what are they?"

"What are what?" asked Eudora.

Tuck handed her the photograph. It was sharp and clear, and it showed, peeping from beneath the screen, a shiny round black lump, and a long, slipperlike thing, just discernible from the shadowed place behind the screen and under the army cot where Eudora was seated.

"Wait a minute!" Tuck said. "I think I know." He put back his head and gave a soundless laugh, like the laugh of a satyr. Then he sobered and looked at Eudora with eyes that were almost sad. "Well, we've found something missing. Something that was here, and isn't now. A pair of black rubbers."

Eudora's spine tingled. "Black rubbers!" she gasped.

"But a good many people wear rubbers," objected Tuck. "I'm afraid you're making a rather wild connection between this lunatic you saw at the insane asylum on the day of the murder, and the rubbers that are missing from this room."

"Phone the asylum!" Eudora shouted. And added, "I dare you to!"

A few mintues later Tuck emerged from the phone booth in the Wagon Wheel, his long face very grave. "Your guess wasn't so wild at that, Miss York. A lunatic did escape from the asylum on Thursday, June ninth, and he was wearing a pair of black rubbers when he was last seen."

Chapter Twenty-one: RECONSTRUCTION (THEORETICAL)

EUDORA SWUNG high the lid of the turtle of her car. "There! Plenty of room and he wasn't a large man."

"But how do we know he left the asylum in *your* turtle?" asked Tuck.

"We don't. That's not the point," Eudora said. "The point is that the convertible coupé, with its nice, roomy turtle, is as common among college students as—as sweaters and fraternity pins. Any car would have served. But my turtle was unlocked. He could easily have seen me stow my books in, and just let the lid drop shut. Wait a sec! I have an idea."

She disappeared into the girl's dormitory, in front of which her tan convertible was parked, and returned in scarcely any time at all with two thick textbooks. "He would have had to prop it open, somehow, to get air," she explained. She propped a book upright at each side of the turtle, where the lid would come down and join the body of the car. Then she closed the lid The two books held it open by several inches "See!" she said.

Froody said gloomily, "He'd of breathed enough exhaust fumes to kill an elephant.'

"But it didn't kill him!" Eudora pointed out. She gestured at the turtle. "No dead body, as you can see. And a pair of rubbers in the prop room." She saw Tuck's face and added, "I'm going with you. Don't say no, because if you do, I'll follow in my car anyhow, and that would be a great waste of gas."

Eudora and Tuck and Froody went swiftly along the cement walk leading to the main building of the insane asylum. Here and there on the wide lawn a group of decorous figures walked, chaperoned by men in white. Beside the walk a gray-haired man in white was talking with a busy little woman in a shapeless black dress, who was busily cutting red roses from one of the bordering bushes.

"Good morning," said the gray-haired doctor, stepping forward. "Isn't it a lovely day?"

Eudora recognized Dr. Flower, the head of the asylum. "We've come to see you," she said. "This is Lieutenant Tuck, and Mr. Froody of the Los Angeles Homicide Squad."

"Dr. Flower," said Tuck, "we've come to talk to you about the patient who escaped."

Dr. Flower nodded. "I'm rather worried about him. We notified the local authorities. He should have turned up before this. He had only something like a dollar and a half in his pocket, and you can't live on that."

Eudora couldn't contain herself. "He *was* the man who was mowing the lawn. A little man, wearing rubbers?"

Dr. Flower turned his calm gray eyes to her face, and it was somehow shocking to realize that they were really little different from the gray eyes of the man with the lawnmower. "Why, yes," said Dr. Flower. "He was." Seeing the look which Eudora and Tuck exchanged, he said, "Come to my office. I see we have some talking to do."

Dr. Flower perched himself on the edge of his desk. "Now tell me," he said, "why the Los Angeles Homicide Squad is interested in Clyde Billings."

"On Thursday night, June ninth," said Tuck, "a young woman was struck on the head and killed at Southwest University. We have just learned that a pair of black rubbers was in the room where she was killed, on the night she died. Miss York has made a connection between them and an inmate she saw here on Thursday afternoon, when she came as a member of Dr. Brewer's class in Abnormal Psychology. I want to know all about Clyde Billings."

Dr. Flower jumped down from the desk and went to a metal filing case. He slid open a drawer and withdrew a folder, from which he took a sheet of paper. He handed it to Tuck. "Here is his case history, the material for which was obtained from him and his family while he was under observation in the Psychiatric Ward at the Los Angeles General Hospital. That's a good beginning."

He sat on the desk while Tuck read the case history, Eudora and Froody crowding him from each side in order to read it too:

Male 20 yrs. of age. Unmarried. Student. Health fair. Claims that for seven years prior to admission to the Psychiatric Ward he had been persecuted by his mother. This persecution, he states, arose from her jealousy of his talent as a pianist. The mother is a concert pianist of note. Asked for particulars, he says he became suspicious of his mother when she refused to allow him to practice as often as he wished. Mother says this is quite true, that he was overdoing it and undermining his general health. He states that his mother's next attempt to smother his genius took place when she insisted that he spend a summer at a boys' camp, where there was only a very poor piano, and where he was not allowed sufficient time for practice because of a number of outdoor activities. Mother states that this action also arose out of anxiety over his health. At the age of 19 he entered a large coeducational university in Los Angeles, where he was not popular. He says that this unpopularity arose out of the jealousy of his classmates. This did not bother him, because he knew he was the greatest pianist in the world, and that genius is always misunderstood. Just before he went home for summer vacation, he was called to the office of the Dean of Men. The Dean told him that he had consulted with his mother about his poor grades in every study except music, and his poor orientation into college life, and that they had agreed that his music courses, of which he was taking the maximum allowed to Freshmen, would be curtailed, and that next year he would be required to join one of the fraternities, if possible. This action, he states, caused him to become very angry with his mother. When he returned home, he accused her of jealousy, they had a violent argument, which resulted in an attempt on his part to strangle her, because of which she had him sent to the hospital for observation. Observation there indicates no mental deterioration; intelligence well preserved; considers other patients insane.

As Tuck laid the case history on the desk, Dr. Flower picked it up and returned it to the folder. "After he had remained in the Hospital for a week, his case was decided by a judge of the Superior Court, one of whose regular duties is to determine whether such people should go to an insane asylum. These sessions are held informally, the only people present being the judge himself, a clerk, the responsible person who caused the patient to come under observation, the psychiatrists from the hospital, the social worker who prepared the case history, and any witnesses of antisocial conduct on the patient's part.

"The psychiatrists' decision was that Billings was a case of pure paranoia, with a clinically fixed suspicion of his mother, an attendant persecutory delusion, and a grandiose delusion with regard to his musical ability. They recommended that he be institutionalized in order that help might be given him. To this the mother reluctantly concurred, and the judge's decision was that of the psychiatrists.

"Billings came here four years ago. Since this asylum is semiprivate, and since his unhappiness without his music was acute, an unused room was soundproofed, his piano was brought, and he has continued his musical studies. He is actually a good musician—I have enjoyed several of his concerts. He is not, of course, the greatest musician in the world, which he still believes. His conduct has been good. His only resentment was shown when we had to insist on exercise for the sake of his health. His own regime was so sedentary that constipation and poor appetite resulted."

"That's why he was mowing the lawn!" cried Eudora.

"Yes. We tried all sorts of games and finally decided to give him a task to do. He had been gardening for a week before he escaped."

"Why did he run away?" asked Tuck. "His existence seems fairly idyllic to me."

"The nurse in charge tells me that he had of late made remarks to the effect that his talent was now ready for the world. I didn't know of that, or he would have been watched more closely."

"Could he have killed this girl?" asked Tuck.

"I don't know the circumstances well enough to say. But if she appeared to him to be a threat to his liberty, he might have struck her. She might have reminded him too strongly of his mother, against whom, by the way, he has never relinquished his hatred. And then, there is a streak of perversion apparent in most cases of paranoia. Persecutory paranoia is often the means by which a person defends himself against a perverse impulse which has become too powerful. In Clyde's case, I suspect an incestuous love of his mother, corroborated by the facts that she is an extraordinarily beautiful woman, and that his delusion appeared at the critical time of puberty. His delusion would serve to mask the love with hate. There may have been a transference of his hatred of her to a hatred of all beautiful women."

"Ann Laird was very pretty," said Eudora.

Dr. Flower glanced at her without seeming to see her. "That's just a suggestion, of course. What I'm getting at is that if he killed her, there was some motive for it, and probably one tied in with his basic delusion. Now, what indication do you have that he did kill her?"

"Very little," said Tuck. "Chiefly the fact that a pair of rubbers were in the room where the crime occurred; that the door of the room opened onto the campus and was either unlocked or half-open during the entire evening and so could have been easily entered; and chiefly that someone returned and took away the rubbers, breaking a window to do so. That suggests guilt to me; a desire to leave no trace which might point to him."

"That's bad," agreed Dr. Flower.

"That's good," said Froody at the same moment.

"Oh, and one more fact," said Dr. Flower. "Clyde was a student at Southwest University when he was institutionalized." He looked at Eudora. "That was four years ago. Before your time, I think."

Eudora only nodded in reply. She was thinking of the homecoming of Clyde Billings. She saw him creeping from the turtle of a car, stretching his cramped muscles, seeing again the red brick buildings which he knew so well. She saw him walking, a stranger and a ghost, across the green lawns of the little world where he had spent his last year of freedom. At first he must have been a little frightened before he realized that in his gray sweat shirt he was wearing the most common kind of campus undress, and was therefore unremarkable.

"Did he smoke?" asked Tuck.

"Yes."

"What brand?"

"Luckies."

"There's something else," Tuck said slowly. "The day after this girl's death, the advertisement of a coffin was torn roughly from a newspaper and stuck with chewing gum to a bulletin board next to the photograph of the dead girl, who had the leading part in the show which the bulletin board was touting. Could Billings have done that?"

"Yes. Billings had a peculiar sense of humor. This sense of humor had no tie-in with his paranoia; it was an extra oddity. I remember that an epileptic woman had a narcoleptic attack. She fell in a deep coma on the lawn. The attendant in charge was some distance away; before he reached her, Clyde came past and saw her lying there. He went quite deliberately to a lily bed near by, picked a flower and laid it on her chest. He was smiling as he did this. When the attendant questioned him as to the reason for his action, he said, 'She looked so damned dead, didn't she?'"

"Oh," said Tuck.

"He also took a peculiar delight in tormenting the other patients, on whom he looked down because he thought himself perfectly sane. When an opportunity presented itself, he would use one of the phones here to call his mother long distance and threaten her life. He's a cold person, and his sense of humor is not a pleasant one."

"I see," said Tuck. "Does he chew gum?"

"Yes," said Dr. Flower, somewhat at a loss.

As they drove back to the campus, Eudora talked. "It all fits!" she exulted. "Those were Luckies you found beside the bench."

"A very popular brand—" said Tuck.

"Don't quibble! Look. Billings got out of my car. He probably waited until after dark. Then he probably got something to eat. He must have been very tired from his ride—I'm not a particularly smooth driver, and I bet he was jolted around a good bit. So he looked for a place to lie down. He thought at once of that deserted, wooded space between Old College and the Ad Building. No one crosses it; it's a dead end, because the wall of the practice field blocks it off at the back. All right. He lay down on the bench and smoked those Luckies you found. Then he noticed the half-open door of the prop room. He probably knew where it led. He investigated and saw the army cot. He must have smiled at his good fortune; he went in, lay down, taking off his rubbers, which were hot and heavy. He wouldn't know, remember, that a play was going on, and that the prop room was in use. Then what happened? He awoke. The light was on. And Ann Laird, a pretty woman, was staring at him. She probably asked him who he was, and what he was doing there, because she would have known he was not a drama student, and therefore had no business in the prop room. Maybe he tried to give her a plausible explanation. Perhaps it didn't satisfy her. She turned to go, and he struck her."

"What with?"

"I don't know. Hey! Maybe with that brass vase! It's weighted with lead!"

"It would sound like a gong being struck," Tuck commented.

"But who would have heard? So then he went away from there fast."

"After turning her over on her back," put in Tuck.

"He could have the idea of making it look like an accident as well as a sane man, remember. There's nothing wrong with his intelligence. It was excitement and fear of discovery that made him turn out the light. Anyone could have done that, too."

"How about the attack on you?"

Eudora frowned. "I'm not so sure about that. And I should think that he would have gone back for the rubbers the same night. He could have got them easily then, because the door wasn't locked until nine-thirty the next morning, when Brewer took over."

"It's obvious why he didn't go back that night," said Tuck. "He had no way of knowing that the body wouldn't be discovered before morning. For all he knew, the room would be full of people, and he couldn't risk being nabbed. He returned the next morning for them, probably, and found the door locked. But why the coffin ad?"

"He bought a paper to read with breakfast. He saw the coffin ad, and it recalled to him the girl lying dead. But why did he go back to Old College? I should think he would have stayed as far from there as possible."

"By daylight he was safer. The night before, lurking

outside the prop room where a dead body lay, he would be a suspicious figure. By day, in his unremarkable getup, he could wander about unobserved. He hoped, probably, to hear students talking and learn whether or not the murder had passed as accident."

"Good!" said Eudora. "So then he saw the dead girl's picture; he had the newspaper under his arm, he remembered the coffin ad, and he was chewing gum. His odd sense of humor asserted itself, and he hastily gummed up the ad. It happened between classes, when the porch would be as deserted as a tomb. Then he was overcome by a desire to know more about the girl he had killed—a morbid curiosity that would go hand-in-hand with what we know about his 'cold' mind. He went to the Student Union —he would know all about the section-card files, they've been there since the year one—and looked up Ann Laird. He got her name of course from the bulletin board. Lo, she has a husband. Again his cruel, tormenting streak comes to the fore. He dials the phone number on the card, gets the husband, tells him his wife is dead. His egocentric streak impelled him to add that he—no one else in the world, mind you, just Clyde Billings—knew who had killed her."

"But how did he get *your* name? You weren't on that convenient bulletin board. Yet he telephoned you at the dormitory to use you as a cat's-paw to get the key to the room where his rubbers were."

"The newspaper story! It appeared Saturday morning, and gave my name, and the fact that I was a drama student. It also gave your name, Mr. Tuck. So Billings knew that as a drama student I would very likely have access to the key to the prop room. He also knew that, since I found the body, I must have been already questioned by you, and would therefore not think it odd if you asked me for further help."

Tuck nodded. "And now I see for the first time why

Meg Fife was struck," he said. "After hitting you on the head, Miss York, he went through your pocket for the key. In doing so, he turned you over, and had a good look at your face. He recognized you as the girl who had seen him at the asylum, and in whose car—we think—he had escaped. And especially as the girl who would be able to make just the connection you have made between him and the rubbers. He knew you had noticed them, because you told me that your roommate commented on them quite loudly. I think, Miss York, that you owe Oliver Clarey your life. If he hadn't passed whistling at nine o'clock last Sunday night, you would probably be dead today."

"Yes," said Eudora thinly.

"Back to Billings. While he was waiting for you, he probably noticed those two little windows, which had not registered in his mind at the time of the murder, and cursed himself for having done the thing the hard way. He didn't know at what moment you might arrive, however, and couldn't risk being caught halfway into the prop room. So he waited and hit you instead. No key. So the next night he came back, broke the window and got the rubbers. It was raining. He put them on and walked away as inconspicuous as ever. Then he saw a figure in a yellow slicker. To him, that meant you, Miss York, and you were dangerous. I strongly suspect that he was the figure who passed Miss Fife under those distorting yellow sodium lights. He had no way of knowing whether he was recognized or not. For all he knew, you had recognized him instantly, and out of fear had forced yourself to walk casually past him, intending to phone the police. So I think he turned and followed you, or rather, Meg Fife. And his worst fears were realized when the yellow raincoat turned into the wing of the Administration Building where the phone booths were. He sneaked in after her, and probably used the handle of his umbrella to deliver a good solid blow to the side of Fife's head. Then, to his astonishment, he saw that he had hit a stranger. I think that must have been a very confusing moment. I think he went away, but fast."

"I wonder where he got the umbrella," said Eudora. "And Meg Fife said the man she met had on a dark suit."

"That," said Tuck, "doesn't bother me. If you had heard, as I have, Miss York, eight witnesses to a crime describe the villain in eight different ways! The only reason I accept the umbrella is that it would have made a handy weapon. As a matter of fact, he may not have had an umbrella at all. Miss Fife may have imagined that he did, because he had on rubbers and it was a rainy night. And umbrellas are easy to swipe."

"And that explains the whole blooming mess," said Froody, with satisfaction. "We've solved everything."

"Except one thing," said Tuck. "Where is Mr. Billings now?"

Chapter Twenty-two: SUGAR FOR FLIES

FINALS BEGAN the next day. All during that hurried week of gulping last scraps of information and regurgitating them on test papers, Eudora daily expected to hear from Ames, and was daily disappointed. *He knows it's exam time, and that I'm too busy to see him,* she reassured herself. But she kept recalling the abrupt way he had turned and left her the night the balcony fell.

When the following week came and went without a phone call from him, Eudora began to be really uneasy. *I do owe him an explanation,* she decided at eleven o'clock Saturday morning, two weeks after the balcony incident. *After all, I did jump at a good many conclusions.* Her eye fell on a copy of the *Life of Beethoven,* which she had noticed one evening when she was having dinner at his house and had asked to borrow. She had forgotten to take it, and the next morning he had driven clear in to the campus to bring it to her. *He can be very sweet,* she thought.

Quickly, before her decision could desert her, she snatched the book from her desk and ran down to her car.

Three quarters of an hour later she turned a bend in the canyon and saw Ames's convertible coming toward her fast. Because both were infringing on the other's lane, Eudora clamped down on the brake. She heard Ames's tires squeal, and the two cars came to a stop nose to nose. A warmth flooded Eudora as she realized that Ames had been on his way to her.

"Hello!" she called. "I was on my way to return *Beethoven.*"

"Oh, that's your book," Ames replied. "I bought it for you." He smiled pleasantly, shifted into reverse and backed his car over to his side of the road. He shifted into low, and the long black hood seemed to leap past her. With her smile stiff and forgotten on her face, she turned her head and watched him vanish around a bend.

Eudora turned slowly back to the wheel. No thoughts were in her mind at all, simply a blind confusion. This was replaced by a single resolve. She worked madly to turn the car, and started after Ames. She caught up with him at the signal at the foot of the canyon, where it emptied into a wide boulevard. "Where are you going?" she yelled.

He half-turned in his seat and called carelessly, "To lunch. Our cook just left us for an aircraft factory. She wants to make bombers instead of biscuits."

The signal turned green; he motioned for a left turn and shot down the boulevard. She followed. He turned in, several miles down, where half a dozen cars nuzzled the low building like pigs around a sow.

She drove in alongside and stopped her car. "Would you care to have lunch with me?" asked Ames.

"Yes, thanks," said Eudora.

A waitress in red slacks brought them menus.

"A ham sandwich and a glass of milk," said Eudora.

"The young lady wishes a ham sandwich and a glass of milk," said Ames to the waitress, who was between the two cars looking dubiously from one to the other. "I will have a hamburger, with onions, and coffee."

She jotted furiously in her pad and departed.

"Did you enjoy the book?" asked Ames.

"Very much. He was a wonderful man."

"The death scene was perfect. How else, after all, could Beethoven have died, except in the middle of a violent thunderstorm, shaking his fist at the heavens?"

"It makes you suspect the historian who chronicled it."

"Does it? I didn't feel that way."

"Were you by any chance on your way to the dormitory?" asked Eudora.

"No."

"Oh."

"Goethe had an interesting death, too," said Ames. "He died saying, 'More light.' In German, of course."

"Naturally," said Eudora. "And there's been so much argument about what he meant. *Mehr licht*, muse the scholars, and evolve theories as to just exactly what he meant. I think it quite possible that if he'd had more strength he might have said, 'For the love of heaven, open a window, it's getting dark in here.'"

"I don't," said Ames.

Conversation lapsed.

"I don't see why you're acting so queerly," Eudora said, and was horrified to hear a voice utterly unlike her own. A small voice, with no backbone to it.

"Am I?" asked Ames. "Ah. Our sandwiches."

Eudora found that her appetite had deserted her. By the time she had nibbled away half the sandwich and swallowed her glass of milk with a great effort, Ames

honked for the waitress and asked Eudora very cour-
teously if she cared for dessert.

"No, thank you."

"Dieting?" asked Ames. "You really shouldn't. You're
a bit on the thin side as it is."

"I am not dieting," said Eudora distinctly. "I find that
my gorge has risen, that's all."

"The young lady doesn't care for anything more," said
Ames to the waitress. "I'll have a piece of pumpkin pie.
With whipped cream."

He ate the pie with enjoyment, wiped his lips on a large
paper napkin, honked for the waitress, paid their bill,
turned the ignition key, started the car, and said, "So
long, Eudora. Give my regards to Freud."

"Well," said Froody. "I think I've just seen Clyde Billings." He was puffing a trifle, and as he sank into the
chair beside Tuck's desk he fanned himself with his limp
black hat. "I'm not sure. I never did think that nuts which
were also killers went around drooling off of their fangs,
but he's the nicest-looking little guy."

"Where did you see him?"

"Like you said. I been making a round of the music
shops, asking after anyone of his general description.
Which is plenty general. Well, I was at this one place on
Hollywood Boulevard, where they also sell tickets to concerts, and while I was talking to the man in charge, a little
guy in a dark blue suit comes in and asks if they have any
general admission tickets to the concert tonight at the
Hollywood Bowl. He says no, you get those through the
box office out there, and the guy goes away. Just when he
came in, the guy in charge was telling me about some
suspicious fellow who was in the day before, and I was all
ears, and then it kind of hit me that the man who just left
was the right size and color, and on top of that I see one
of those Bowl posters, and I see that a guy named Horo-

witz is featured for tonight, and that rings a bell, and so I ask the music shop guy who Horowitz is, and he looks at me like I have two or three heads and says, 'One of the greatest living pianists.' That means piano_player."

"Yes," said Tuck. "I know. So when you reached the street, the man who inquired about a ticket to the Bowl tonight was out of sight."

"Yeah." Froody examined the lining of his hat with unconvincing absorption. Then he looked up at Tuck out of his sad, bulging eyes. "Now don't be mad at me."

Tuck reached out and patted Froody's shoulder. "Mad? Why, I'm going to take you to a concert."

When Eudora opened the door of their room, Millicent was looking into the mirror. She turned her head, which wore the tight crimp of a new wave, and smiled—stiffly and experimentally. Her braces were gone.

"Oh, grand!" said Eudora, putting deliberate gladness into her voice, for fear that even surprise would not rob it of a certain drab quality. "You sly devil! You didn't tell me you were going to have 'em taken off."

"I wasn't sure the dentist would do it. I put up a good fight. I told him they were warping my ego."

"What did he say to that?"

"He just grunted. But he took them off. And guess what else?"

"You're marrying the star quarterback tomorrow."

Millicent shook her head. "No. I turned him down. I told him I don't like muscle men."

Eudora hugged her. "Baby, you've got a sense of humor!"

Millicent said solemnly, "I'm trying to develop one. Oh, Eudora, I wish I'd had this done a long time ago." She looked at her reflection in the mirror, sadly. Then she tilted her head and again gave that tentative smile.

"Well, what else?" asked Eudora, flinging herself across

the bed.

Millicent spun around. "Oh! Well, after I left the dentist, I went to my aunt's, and—she has the flu!" She saw Eudora's doubtful look and added, "She was giving a theater party tonight and had to call it off, so she gave me the tickets. And I've already invited six people and four have accepted!"

"Who did you ask?"

"Paul and Meg and Oliver Clarey and Jim. And I asked Dave Draska and his Lily, but Dave said they couldn't come." She lowered her eyelids. "Jim was really very nice, but he sounded sad, and when I explained why I'd called I was sure he would refuse so I told him I would understand, and he said he thought maybe some good music was just what he needed, and oh, he was so *nice.*"

"How many tickets did your aunt give you, anyway?"

"Eight. Well, that makes four, and you're five, and I'm six, and that's only two wasted."

"You didn't ask Ames, then, for me?"

"No. I asked Oliver. I've given up about you and Ames. And I think you're crazy, Eudora. He really likes you, and he's tried so hard, and I think you've been awfully mean to him."

Eudora looked down at her hands and noticed irrelevantly that her nails needed filing. "Well, why don't you phone him?" she asked.

"You mean you want to go with Ames?"

"That's right."

Millicent's face showed confusion. "But—"

Eudora jumped up from the bed. "Let's phone now. Don't say you've talked with me. Just say you're giving a party at the Bowl and of course want him to come. Make it plain that you've already bought a ticket for him, so he'll be less likely to back out."

"Back *out!* Say, what's happened between you two?"

"Come on," said Eudora. "Let's phone."

She found herself walking up and down the hall while Millicent dialed Ames's number, and the housekeeper said she would see if he was home. Finally Millicent said, "Ames?" And Eudora was beside the phone, her ear as close as possible to the receiver.

"Yes. Who's this?"

"This is Millicent, Ames. I'm having a theater party tonight and of course am expecting you. . . . Now don't say no, because I've already got the tickets, and I'll be terribly disappointed if you don't come."

Eudora stiffened.

"Gosh, but I'm sorry," said Ames. "As a matter of fact, I've made other plans for this evening, and so—"

Millicent rolled doleful eyes up at Eudora. Eudora snatched the receiver, and Millicent did a neat sidestep, and in turn bent her ear to the receiver.

"Ames!" said Eudora. "Who do you think you are, going somewhere? You be here for me tonight at seven, or I'll never speak to you again!"

Millicent clapped her small hand over the mouthpiece. "Sugar catches more flies," she whispered fiercely, and withdrew her hand.

Eudora swallowed. She took a deep breath. "Please?" she cooed.

There was a silence. "Seven sharp," said Ames.

Chapter Twenty-three: IN THE GREAT BOWL

WALKING UP the steep ramp from the highway to the Hollywood Bowl, Eudora forgot the constraint between them in Ames's car and gave herself up to coming pleasure. The long fronds of a lane of pepper trees touched her hair as she passed beneath them, and swung idly in the light that burst out of the Bowl restaurant where dishes clattered, a ticket office where a short queue of people waited. Eudora found that she and Ames were fighting the slope with the same rhythmic, slow strides. He must have noticed too, because he looked down at her and then away.

Millicent had arranged that they all would meet in front of the refreshment booth, just beyond the entrance where an attendant took the tickets; Millicent, Jim and Oliver were already there. Millicent, dressed in pale blue, was standing between the two men, and when she saw Eudora and Ames she came forward with her new, careful smile. "Hello," she said brightly. "Now there's just Meg and Paul. You know, someone should have picked them up. Neither of them has a car. I'm afraid I arrange things very clumsily."

"You arrange things very cleverly," said Ames.

"I don't believe you all know each other," said Millicent quickly. "Ames Hanna—Jim Laird and Oliver Clarey." The men shook hands, and then Millicent waved frantically. Eudora turned and saw Paul and Meg coming up the sloping walk. Paul looked small and neat in a dark suit. Meg was hatless and had on a bright red coat. "How nice you look together," said Millicent.

"We know it," Paul replied with his small smile.

"You know Jim Laird. I think," said Millicent.

"Sure," said Paul. "How are you, Laird?"

"Fine," said Jim quietly.

"And this is Ames Hanna—Meg Fife and Paul Ober. Oh, dear. I did that backward. Well—let's go. . . ."

At the turnstile leading into the Bowl, Eudora was startled to see Tuck and Froody and another man whom she belatedly recognized. in his street clothes, as Dr. Flower. Tuck saw her at the same moment and woodenly raised his hat.

The Hollywood Bowl always made Eudora think of a Roman amphitheater. greatly magnified. Tier after tier of people swept around in a vast semicircle; below them the quarter globe of the shell glowed with gold-green light as cool and clean as the sound of flutes. The musicians were taking their places like tiny black puppets.

Everywhere people chattered and milled and followed grimly hurrying ushers to their seats. A group passed Eudora laden with plaid robes and cushions, as though going camping. A sweet little old man, who looked exactly like an aged violinist and who was probably a plumber, wandered toward them, humming.

"You love this, don't you?" asked Ames. "So do I."

"That gives us something in common, then, doesn't it?" said Eudora.

Ames started to press her arm and apparently thought better of it.

Their seats, which were not seats, but most of a long bench, were good. Halfway up and square in the center. Meg went in first, then Paul. Oliver followed, holding Millicent by the hand. She started to draw back and looked over her shoulder toward Jim, who was looking out at the surrounding hills.

Ames glanced at him and followed Millicent. Eudora sat next to Ames and reached out gently and tugged at Jim's sleeve. He turned his bemused face down at her, grinned and seated himself at the end of the bench.

The muted dissonance of tuning instruments reached them like a promise of what was to come. "I got some programs while we were waiting," she heard Millicent say. "Pass one down, Ames." Ames handed her a program and she opened it, turning so that the glow from one of the high, powerful lights would fall on it.

The first half of the concert consisted of the *Appassionata,* the *Emperor Concerto,* and, presumably to give Mr. Horowitz a rest, the *Romeo and Juliet* overture.

She looked quickly to see if Jim had been glancing at the program over her shoulder, but he was still looking at the hills. One star had trembled into life, she saw. Then applause spattered and grew into a steady volume of sound as the conductor crossed the stage. He bowed and motioned Horowitz from the wings.

The applause grew even louder, died quickly away; there was a pregnant silence in which the sharp sound of someone lighting a match just behind Eudora was abnormally loud. Then the music began, coming fine and clear to her ears from the shell's wide mouth, enveloping her in waves of sound from a mind long stilled.

For no reason at all, into Eudora's mind flashed the remembrance of Tuck, woodenly raising his hat. Suddenly she knew those three quiet men had waited at the entrance for Clyde Billings, who thought he was the greatest pianist in the world. Clyde Billings might have come earlier than they had, in order to get the best possible seat, and might at this moment be hearing the same note of music she was hearing. The thought was oddly unsettling. For a moment, only her ears listened to the *Appassionata*. Her mind went with her eyes, following the wide curve of people on each side, row upon row sloping down toward the shell below her, wondering whether among all these men and women might not be sitting one small man, murderous and mad, also listening.

The minute black figure at the piano played and moved as he played; and from all the rolling grassy acres about them came the steady sound of crickets, asserting their prior right to this cleft in the hills.

She looked at Ames. He listened as she did, his eyes watching the musicians, or roving the throng to catch the quick little flares of matches being lighted. She turned her head and looked at Jim Laird. Both arms were spread wide over the back of the bench. His eyes were shut, and his head drooped. He must have become aware of her, because he raised his head and smiled, and his smile was stiff and sad. He reached into his pocket and offered her a cigarette with a mute raising of his blond brows. She shook her head. He drew one from his pack, put the pack into his side pocket, reached for matches, and cupped the flame in his hands. The ruddy light warmed his face and brightened the arc of light hair hanging over his square forehead. She suddenly thought how often Ann's small thin hand must have reached quickly forward in one of her impetuous gestures to smooth that lock into place.

When the *Romeo and Juliet* overture began, Ames whispered, "They ought to turn this dear old thing out to pasture." She gave his mild witticism a quick smile and was abruptly aware of a change in Jim Laird. Under her eyelashes she saw that he was sitting very straight, looking unblinkingly down at the gold glow of the shell where the tiny black figures sawed and blew. Even through Ames's insulating bulk, she could feel the other's awareness of what was being played, and what it meant for them. Millicent's small chin was quivering; she was strained forward with round glittering eyes. Clarey's dark face, with its eternal smudge of beard, was deliberately, remotely somber. For a moment she felt he was overacting. She leaned still farther forward and saw Paul looking steadily up at a star; Meg, her pointed face a pallid blue in the light from the shell, had her eyes on a handkerchief in her red lap, from which she was slowly tearing the hem.

The man in front of Jim Laird lighted a match. That swung her gaze in that direction. Someone was standing at the end of their row—someone who had come very silently. Jim was still sitting straight, watching the miniature musicians far below. The man standing at the end of the bench was a small man in a dark suit. She recognized him at once as Clyde Billings. He was looking down at Jim Laird, and on his face was a look of power, a triumphant look that showed itself in a tiny, icy smile. Then Jim turned his head toward Billings. Billings leaned forward a few inches and said in a low voice, "I need more money, Laird."

Millicent's little voice asked, "Who is it, Jim?"

Jim Laird stood up. His back was to Eudora, and she saw for the first time how broad his shoulders were. He just stood there for an endless moment. Then he seemed to grow, literally got taller. His voice was coarse and hard as he said, "Get outa my way!"

Billings tilted his head ever so slightly and stepped aside so that he was standing in the aisle at the end of the row below them. Jim started up the steps. The little man followed him and laid a hand on his arm. Jim Laird spun around, put the palm of his hand flat on Billings' chest, and shoved hard; he at once turned and continued on his way. She heard, quite clearly, the dull thump as Billings' head hit the end of a bench, across the aisle and three rows down.

Chapter Twenty-four: OF THESE SAD THINGS

EUDORA'S FEET made great echoes in the marble corridor. She heard someone whistling, and a man rounded a corner ahead of her. "Please," she called. "Where is the Homicide Squad?" He stopped whistling long enough to say, "You turn to your left, see? Then you go clear to the end, see? Then you turn right, and it's the third door down. See?"

"Clearly," said Eudora. "All I need is a compass." But she followed his instructions and was not a little surprised to find a door on which was lettered: *Homicide Squad.* She opened it, and directly ahead of her was a big desk at which sat a fat man with graying hair and a look of chronic irritation. "I'm Captain Gufferty," he said, in a hoarse voice. "What can I do for you?"

"I want to see Lieutenant Tuck," said Eudora, expecting almost any reaction.

Captain Gufferty pointed with a blunt forefinger at a door to his right. "In there," he said.

She turned into a large room full of desks and saw Tuck

sitting at one of them. "Oh," he said. "You."

Eudora sat down on the chair beside his desk. "I want to know what goes on. I want to know everything."

"Laird killed his wife," said Tuck. "He gave her a shove —just the kind of shove you saw him give Billings. She hit her head on the dumbbell beside the table." He went on examining the rope.

She poked him. "Why?" she asked.

He sighed. He got up and went into the outer office. She heard Gufferty's hoarse voice: "What do you want?"

"The stuff on the Laird case. Is it in here?"

"Yeah." There was the metallic rumble of the drawer of a filing case being opened. Tuck returned with some long papers, which he handed to her. "He and Billings were both questioned down here last night. There's the result."

Tingling with excitement, Eudora began to read. Billings' statement was on top, so she read that first:

QUESTION: Did you escape from the asylum in one of the students' cars parked out front?

ANSWER: Yes. I hid in the turtle. No one saw me.

Q: Please tell in your own words what happened.

A: I saw two women get out of a car. I saw one of them raise the lid of the turtle. That gave me my idea. I'd wanted to get away. I'm not insane, and I—

Q: We know all about that. Please go on.

A: I waited until they were all in the building. Then I hid. There were two books in the turtle. After I heard the women get into the car again, I propped the lid open with the books. We stopped once. Then we got to campus. I heard both doors slam. I was afraid they'd come around for the books, but they didn't. So I waited until it was nearly dark. Then I climbed out.

Q: You recognized your surroundings?

A: Are you kidding? I went to school there for a year. Of course I did.

Q: Go ahead.

A: We were parked right in front of a café. So I went in and bought a hamburger and a cup of coffee. I was plenty tired. I had a headache. I wanted some sleep. I wandered around, kind of getting my bearings, and I saw that the best place for me to go was that spot between Old College and the Ad Building. I found me a nice long bench under a tree, and I lay down. I smoked a while. The bench was pretty hard. I saw this door half open, and I thought, *Clyde, old boy, let's see where this goes to.* So I got up and went over and opened it. I saw it was the room where they store theatrical junk. I lit a match and there was a nice cot straight ahead of me, with a blanket and everything. So I closed the door and went over and lay down. Oh, and I took off these rubbers I had on. But it was plenty hot in there. No ventilation. I decided the bench was better. So I went outside again. And this time I went to sleep.

Q: What time was this?

A: How the hell would I know? Do you see any gold wristwatches on me?

Q: Go ahead, please.

A: After a while I woke up. There was a light shining on my feet. I pulled them in fast and sat up and looked around the tree I was lying under. The door to that junk room was open, and a couple of people were inside. I could see them plain as looking onto a stage.

Q: Who were the people?

A: I didn't know, then. Do you want me to tell you who I found out they were?

Q: Yes.

A: Laird and his wife.

Q: Go ahead, please.

A: They were arguing. The first thing I heard was his voice saying, "I'm not going, Ann, and that's final. I'm fed up with your boobus intelligentsia pals. I'm going home. Here's the key." She grabbed the key and chucked it into her purse. She said she thought he was mean. Then he said some more along the same line—I don't remember all the words, but I remember their voices got louder and louder. Finally she said, "You're my husband, and I have a right to expect you to act like one. I want you to go with me to Carlo's tonight. What are people going to think?" And he said, "And you're my wife, Ann. I have a right to expect some consideration. And I don't give a damn what people think. I'm going home." And he turned and started for the door. His face was in the light for a minute, and what a face! Dead white, like paste, and the lips white too. Then he passed the light and was just a dark shape. She ran up behind him in her white dress. I've never seen bigger, madder eyes. "Don't you dare walk out on me!" she yelled, and grabbed his arm. Then it happened. He spun around and pushed, all in one movement. I heard the crash as she fell. Then he came out fast, and put his hand to the side of his head like it hurt him, and walked fast to the front of the building. He never looked back. From where I was I could only see the girl's feet. She didn't move. I waited behind the tree in case someone heard the noise and was coming to see what was wrong, but no one came. So I went in. She was lying with her head against that iron dumbbell. I lifted her head up and saw she was a goner. So I laid it down on the floor....

Q: You say she was a goner. Was she dead?

A: She looked dead to me. The back of her head was smashed in.

Q: Go on.

A: Someone knocked on the inside door. A woman's voice called, "Ann?" Boy, was I scared! I stood still until I thought she'd gone, and then I tiptoed over and turned the light out. I shut the door and made tracks.

Q: Where did you go?

A: I went to the park, up at the end of campus. There was more chance of being picked up for vagrancy there, but I had to take that chance. But before I went to sleep on the grass, I got an idea. If no one else knew this guy had killed his wife, it would be worth money to him for me to keep my mouth shut.

Q: In other words, you decided to blackmail him.

A: Call it what you want

Q: How did you work it?

A: That happened smooth as glass, kind of like God was on my side. I went down to the drugstore and bought a

paper. I hardly thought the story would be in the paper
yet, but it was worth a nickel to know. No story. So I
went to the same café where I ate dinner and got some
coffee and a doughnut. That left me with ninety-eight
cents. I read the paper, and I kept it to look through the
want ads in case I couldn't get a track on this guy who
killed his wife. I went over to the room where it happened,
but the door was locked. I figured they'd found the body.
Then, as I was passing by the front of the building, I
looked up on the porch and saw this bulletin board. I don't
know what made me go up and look closer, but I did. And
there was this dead girl's picture, and her name. Ann
Laird. No one was around. No one at all.

Q: And you had the paper under your arm. Is that
when you tore out the coffin ad and stuck it to the picture
with chewing gum?

A: That's right.

Q: Why?

A: It seemed kind of funny to me, this picture grinning out and all the time the girl was dead.

Q: I see. Then what did you do?

A: I high-tailed it for the Student Union. I knew her
name, now, you see, and all I had to do was look up her
address, which would also be the address of the husband.

Q: What time was this?

A: I don't know. What difference did that make to
me?

Q: Go on.

A: So then I went to the Union. I got her phone number, too, and went to a booth in the hall of the Ad Building and phoned. When this man answered I said, "Laird?
I know your wife is dead, and I know you killed her."

Q: *You* killed her?

A: Right. He hung up on me. So I gave him time to
think it over and phoned again and told him he better
see me, that I was a friend. He told me how to get to his
house. So I went to see him. I was careful, and kept
plenty of space between us, believe me, but he didn't have
any more fight left in him. "Laird," I said, "I saw it happen. I'm not setting myself to judge anybody. All I want

is some money." "How much money?" he asked, in this dead voice, and I said, "A hundred dollars, and a suit of clothes. You can see I'm not taking advantage of you," I said. "Why should I? I've got a talent, Laird, and when I get going, I'll be able to buy and sell you ten times." So he wrote me a check for a hundred dollars and went into the closet in the bedroom and came out with this dark blue suit. What else could he do?

Q: What did you do then?

A: I got a job playing a piano in a cheap joint in Hollywood. I figured it had to be a cheap joint, or they'd want a member of the Musicians' Union, which I am not. Does that sound crazy? I'm twice as sane as anyone in this room.

Q: Did you hit a young woman named Eudora York on the head?

A: Yes. I was sorry to have to do that. But I got thinking about those damned rubbers. The rain made me think of them. The only way I could think to get them was to use her to bring me the key. I saw her name in the paper. I never noticed those windows until I was waiting for her to show up.

Q: You also hit a woman named Meg Fife.

A: Was that her name? I was sorry to have to do that, too. But I thought she was the girl who saw me, as plain as I see you, up at the asylum. I passed her after I'd broken the window to get my rubbers, and I thought she recognized me. Then after I hit her in the phone booth, it was someone else, in the same kind of yellow raincoat. Boy, did that stop me for a minute.

Q: What did you do then?

A: I went back to Hollywood. Did they think I was crazy? The hell they did! The guy who hired me said I was the best piano player he'd ever had, and he wasn't lying. I'm the best there is. I'm tops. I was doing all right, until you grabbed me going into the Bowl. They used to let me play what I wanted, real music, not this cheap stuff, after the place closed and they were counting the cash. They gave me a place in the back to sleep, and after they'd all gone, and the place was locked up for the night, I'd sit there at that lousy piano and play what I wanted to play, all night long. And God, I can play. Sometimes it frightens me. Then I'd go back to my cot and figure how after they thought I was dead, up there at the asylum, I'd get a better job and go right on up to the top, where I belong.

Eudora folded the stapled sheets together, and tugged at Tuck's sleeve. "I don't understand what happened at the Bowl. If you caught Billings as he was going in, how did he wind up beside Jim Laird halfway through the concert?"

"Oh," said Tuck. "That. Well, as soon as Billings told me Laird had done the killing, I saw I was in a bad spot. Because Laird, if he had any brains at all, would realize that the only voice against him was the voice of a lunatic. He could simply stick to the story of his own innocence, and I wouldn't have much of a case for a jury. So I decided I wanted to see the two men together. I'd seen Laird go in with your party. I told Billings what to say and sent him in after Laird, and sat down two rows back, and Laird came through with a bang."

"Did you arrange to have them play the *Romeo and Juliet* overture too?" asked Eudora?

"No. That was my friend Chance."

Eudora began to read Laird's statement:

Q: Why did you kill your wife?

A: I didn't kill her. I pushed her. It was an accident.

Q: I will rephrase my question. Why did you push your wife with such force that she struck her head and died from the blow?

A: I don't know.

Q: Take all the time you need in answering the question.

A: We were incompatible.

Q: In what way?

A: In all ways.

Q: What did you do after leaving the properties room?

A: I went home. I went to bed. I finally went to sleep. I didn't know she was dead.

Q: But when I told you your wife was dead, you realized that you had killed her?

A: Yes.

Q: And decided to get away with it if you could?

A: Yes. What would you have done?

Q: Why did you go to the prop room?

A: To give her her keys. She'd left them home, on the coffee table, when she raced out to the rehearsal. I knew I'd be asleep when she got home from Carlo's.

Q: What caused the argument between you and your wife?

A: I don't know. Something about Carlo's. I didn't want to go to Carlo's.

Q: Why?

A: I don't like her friends. They talk too much. I don't talk much. I just sit and listen. I was tired of listening to them. Sick to death of it. Because they never said anything worth listening to.

Q: Were there any other differences between you and your wife?

A: (Laughter)

Q: Take all the time you wish in answering.

A: There were so many differences between us that I don't know where to begin. She was an actress first, and a wife second. That was part of it. And I'm an artist first and a husband second. People like that shouldn't marry. We married in haste, and oh, God! did we repent at leisure.

Q: Yet the statement has been made that your wife was deeply in love with you.

A: I could have done with less love and more beefsteak.

Q: Then you no longer loved your wife when you killed her?

A: That night in that prop room I hated her.

Q: I am still at a loss for the reason behind this hate.

A: Look. We married fast. We knew nothing about each other except the best things. Dress-up clothes and dress-up manners. We lived together over a year in a small apartment. We didn't just rub each other the wrong way on some things; we rubbed each other the wrong way on all things. I'm slow—she's fast. I like to sit around at night and read; she likes to talk or go somewhere. I don't like people; she loves people—her fondness for them used to shine out of her sometimes, like a special kind of light. My family likes to go on picnics. She hates picnics. What I'm trying to tell you is that we were polar opposites. It showed even when we walked down a street together. She was always just one step ahead of me, pulling at my arm. Oh, God, how I got to hate that pulling at my arm. Look. I don't express myself very well. I'm not good with words. She was. She could make 'em jump through hoops. What was I saying? Oh. I'm trying to tell you that what happened in the prop room had been coming for almost a year. It had been building up inside me, and finally it broke out. I believe she thought that I was fairly happy, most of the time. But the happiness wore out fast, like a cheap suit, and day by day I grew to hate her, with just little flashes of liking, when the fine things in her showed through all her ways that were different from my ways. What happened was bound to happen. From the minute we turned away from the minister and started up the aisle, Ann going fast, me going slow. It was there, underneath everything, waiting.

Q: How long had you been going together before you married?

A: Three months. She was the strangest woman. There'll never be another like her. She was too much for me. There was never any peace. She didn't like peace. She liked things to happen. Well, she got her wish. Poor kid.

Q: Then for all these reasons you killed her.

A: For all these reasons, I killed her.

Q: Froody. Catch him. He's fainted.

Eudora slowly folded the papers together and laid them on Tuck's desk. "People don't do such things."

Tuck looked up. "Oh, yes, they do."

"Then he's not sane."

"He's perfectly sane."

"I often find myself wondering," said Tuck, "how many tragedies like this go on in the cottages of the world."

"There's some other reason he hasn't told."

"Ann Laird," said Tuck, "was killed, to brief it, because she was a good actress, but a bad cook. She was killed because she didn't ever learn that a wife is wife, mother, nurse, friend, and housekeeper. If she's a good wife, that is. It's too bad, but that's how the world goes round."

"Attraction-repulsion," mused Eudora. "The most striking case I've ever heard of."

"Oh, that, too," said Tuck. "And all the things Laird couldn't find words for."

"What's going to happen to Jim?"

Tuck shrugged. "That will be up to the jury. He'll plead manslaughter, of course. And the jury will have to decide whether Ann Laird was killed by her husband's push, or the iron weight that happened to be lying in just the wrong place, or by a cunning little lunatic who went away and left her to die."

"She wasn't dead when he picked her up?"

"Not a chance. If he'd called a doctor, she might be alive now."

Eudora stood up stiffly.

Tuck rose too. "Now don't go figuring up some fancy motives for Laird. You know the truth, the whole truth, and nothing but the truth."

"You sound very wise," snapped Eudora.

"Well," said Tuck, "I was married once, for five years. I looked at my wife across the breakfast table one morning, and got up and went out, and never came back."

Eudora was very cool and poised. She noticed irrelevantly a small, round grease spot on the minister's cuff.

"I, Eudora, take thee Ames . . . to be my lawful wedded husband, to have and to hold, to love and to cherish . . . in sickness or in health , for better or for worse . . . for richer or for poorer . . . forsaking all others . . . until death us do part."

Made in the USA
Coppell, TX
15 December 2023

26157753R10113